IF I KNEW THE WAY, I WOULD TAKE YOU HOME

IF I KNEW THE WAY,
I WOULD TAKE
YOU HOME

DAVE HOUSLEY

DZANC
BOOKS

5220 Dexter Ann Arbor Rd.
Ann Arbor, MI 48103
www.dzancbooks.org

The following stories originally appeared in these literary magazines:

Be Gene, *Knee-Jerk Review;* The Jerry Garcia Finger, *Quarterly West;* Rockabye, *Hobart* (forthcoming); Death and the Wiggles, *Beloit Fiction Journal;* Pop Star Dead at 22, *Wigleaf* and *Dzanc's Best of the Web 2010;* Goliath, *Stress City: An Anthology of Writing from DC Guys;* Where We're Going, *Summerset Review;* Paul Stanley Summarizes the Tragedies of William Shakespeare During Between Song Banter from the 1977-78 KISS Alive II Tour, *Yankee Pot Roast;* So Fucking Metal, *Heavy Feather Review;* Rock Out, Mate, *Mid-American Review;* How to Listen to Your Old Hair Metal Tapes, *Columbia: A Journal of Art and Literature;* Dim Lights, Thick Smoke, *The Collagist*

Designed by Steven Seighman

Library of Congress Cataloging-in-Publication Data

Housley, Dave, 1967-
  [Short stories. Selections]
  If I Knew the Way, I Would Take You Home : stories / by Dave Housley.
    pages cm
  1. Rock music—Fiction. I. Title.
  PS3608.O86437A6 2015
  813'.6—dc23
                                    2014013389

ISBN: 978-1936873664

First U.S. Edition: January 2015

Printed in the United States of America

10 9 8 7 6 5 4 3 2 1

'Cause these kids at the shows, they'll have kids of their own,
and these sing-a-long songs will be their scriptures.

—CRAIG FINN, THE HOLD STEADY

CONTENTS

LIVE IN CONCERT: STORIES

INTERLUDE: COVER SONG

INTERLUDE: NOVELTY SONG

CONTENTS

IF I KNEW THE WAY, I WOULD TAKE YOU HOME

BE GENE

THE DEMON WIPES HIS BOOTS on the welcome mat and slips in the door as quietly as possible. He takes off one black leather, studded, six-inch platform boot, and then the other. The pair cost two hundred dollars from some shop in London, are purported to be the pair that Gene Himself wore on the UK stretch of the Love Gun tour, 1978, the band's creative and commercial peak. Eddie admires them again as he pauses in the doorway. With their diamond-shaped, bullet-studded plates twinkling in the near dark, they resemble ancient castles, sitting quiet while inside knights prepare for war, feasting and drinking, sharpening swords and spears and daggers, singing songs and making boasts about the battle to come. He thinks about both of those castles. He is old enough to understand that the plans being made in one of them will not come to fruition. He picks up the electric bill, which has been placed unopened and conspicuous on the table, and writes "Twin Castles." As a title, it's not bad at all. Shit, Zeppelin wrote all their songs about The Lord of the Rings, fucking name-checked Mordor in the biggest classic rock power ballad of all time, and Robert Plant isn't worried about the Discover Card bill coming due next week, or how much a ton of mulch runs nowadays, is he?

He removes the matchbook from his pocket. An address, a few miles away, written in Duane's stupid cartoon handwriting. A time. If he is going, he has an hour. He looks down the hallway. As usual, all is dark.

He removes the breastplate and places it on a coat hanger. An eBay purchase—not the real thing, but a perfect replica of the one from the Asylum tour in 1985. A bad vintage, admittedly, but it was cheap and shipping was free and the original piece, back when times were good and they were actually touring, got lost somewhere between Cleveland and Pittsburgh right around the time grunge was putting the final nails into hair metal's coffin.

He tiptoes through the living room, opens the refrigerator. He takes out two hot dogs and places them in the microwave, punches in forty seconds, and walks soundlessly down the hall to the bathroom. He pulls his hair into a ponytail. The cold cream is in the medicine cabinet, next to the pregnancy test kits and the Midol and the Pepto-Bismol. He takes a long pull straight from the Pepto and then rinses the chalky mint out of his mouth with water. He was lucky to make it through the show without needing the bathroom. There was a time when he could eat two dozen chicken wings at a pop. He remembers those nights in DC, opening for Saxon or Leper at the old 9:30 or the Black Cat, then a few lines, maybe ten gin and tonics, no lie, then close out the night with huevos rancheros or a plate of chili-cheese fries and a half smoke. A long time ago.

He regards his face in the mirror: hard lines forming around his eyes, running down toward his nostrils, the whole thing tightening into itself, collapsing and hardening all at once, like a piece of old pottery. He has bass guitars older than the new drummer.

His make-up has run, but he likes the way it came out: gothy streaks extending down from where he caked on the black and ran three hooks up and down, like a bear trap from an old cartoon. He strikes a pose from the *Alive II* album, Gene with pinky and index finger extended into the goat, long tongue wagging like some kind of man-reptile in heat, his black hair sweaty and wild. He wishes his tongue were longer, but he has thought this before, and he is done with real wishes—Christmas lists, brighter tomorrows, lottery tickets. Today is Altoona and the landscaping business and the tendinitis in his Achilles, two gigs a month for Luv Gunzz and Carrie asleep down the hall. The address on the matchbook and Duane, good ex-Marine that he is, cleaning his guns in a car not far from here, watching the clock, waiting.

Duane, who is a terrible Ace Frehley but will do in a pinch. Duane, who is actually good at what he actually does. A thought. A check in one column. He looks at the scrap of paper again. An address. Best not to think too much about it. Any information is too much. If he's going to do it, he needs to look at it like a bad gig, a birthday party or corporate event. You show up, play your role, leave it all on the stage, get out of there with a check in your pocket. If you have the right kind of attitude, then you don't think about it too much—maybe don't think about it at all, until the next time.

The make-up should come off, but he knows he won't do it until later.

Those kids were at the show again tonight. Young, but not too young. College age. Rich kids back for the holidays. This time they brought friends, a whole group of grinning, high-fiving frat boys and sorority girls, all of them done up in tastefully weathered clothes that must have cost as much as a decent guitar, an amplifier newer than the Fender. Luv Gunzz is a tribute band, and he made his peace long ago with all that that means—it's not music so much as a show. People have certain expectations, some baggage that, you look at it in the right kind of light, then, yeah, it looks a little funny, maybe even a little sad. But these kids, they were there for something different. Comedy. A spectacle. If he wasn't a professional, wasn't able to push himself down and bring Gene up, he would have stopped the show and kicked somebody's ass.

He slips outside and pushes his codpiece down until he can wiggle enough room to urinate. His neighbor's houses glow in the dark, soft lights pulsing from kitchens and living rooms. The neighborhood is asleep. Straights. Squares. He is a novelty in this little community of ranch houses, of assistant managers and teachers and housewives. He knows this, and he likes it. Carrie used to like it too. For the longest time, decades, it was the thing that kept them going, their shared joke, a crackle running between them like electricity. There was a time when she never missed a gig, when they would hit the bars together after a show, when she would slink into the changing room, panties already tucked into her purse, and find him before he even had a chance to wipe off the stage sweat.

It's been years since she's been to a show. She's never even met Duane. Probably a good thing. Another check in another column.

He looks out at the manicured lawns stitched together with split rail and French gothic fences, lilacs, azaleas, and rhododendrons. Nice and orderly. But two decades spent trimming and mowing and whacking, mulching and planting and trimming again, have taught him that it is nothing but chaos, a frantic reaching for the sun. Leave it be for a few years and this entire subdivision gets choked into jungle.

Of course, nobody in this neighborhood is hiring the likes of Trim It Up Landscaping. Not anymore. Ever since the country's financial infrastructure blew up like a cheap speaker, everybody found their lawnmower again. Even the old ladies seem to be doing their own planting. The mortgage is due in a week, and the checking account holds three hundred twenty dollars. The gig tonight netted a grand total of three hundred, minus fifty bucks a man, minus twenty for the bar tab.

The hot dogs will be ready to eat. He moves into the living room, unbuckles the codpiece and lets it slide onto the carpet, where it lands with a metallic little *chang.* The codpiece is the real deal. Aged eighteen-gauge steel. Two hundred bucks from some medieval fantasy website. A nearly exact replica of the one Gene Himself wore on

5

the Destroyer tour. As always, he feels exposed without it. Something about the combination of the make-up and the codpiece make him feel huge, powerful, like the God of Thunder. Onstage, he controls everything. No hassles, surprises, bill collectors. No ovulation predictor tests, no Home Depot jacking up the price on grass seed, no garbage and recycling and hedges growing wilder every single day. He writes out a set list and they play it. He stops singing a chorus, holds the microphone out toward the crowd, and they roar. He breathes fire, spits blood, and they cheer. It is like being the director of a play, the conductor of a symphony. It is like being Gene Himself.

This is what Duane likes about him, too—his size and stage presence, the way he can command the scene without saying much. It comes in handy in Duane's actual line of work. "Be Gene," he says. "Don't be Eddie. Be the Demon."

Duane will give him the shotgun, sit back and play Ringo to his Paul and John, keeping everything tight, everything moving along, while Gene points, gestures, waves his gun around, and shouts stage directions—"money and the drugs in the bag! In the bag!"—does everything but hold the microphone out for them to sing along.

He considers the television. Better to let Carrie sleep. Lately, with the hormones, the whole thing with the cycle and the ovulation, sleep is the one thing she doesn't complain about.

The hot dogs are split and steaming. He slathers on mustard and ketchup, skips the bun, and eats them with a fork and knife. Jesus, he thinks, hot dogs no bun. Fucking carbs. One more concession to the band, the role. Nobody is paying to see the KISS from this decade—or the past two, for that matter. They want *Destroyer, Love Gun, Alive II*. The real diehards, they don't even want to hear "Lick It Up," and that was a goddam good song.

Thirty minutes if he's going to meet Duane. If he doesn't go, Duane will just do the job himself. He pictures the scene: a few burnouts with a bag full of money, a package, cutting it up into smaller packages, wearing hospital masks like they learned on television. Duane with a shotgun, a mask. Money and packages change hands. Duane with a bundle of cash. Duane with a few months' rent, car payments for a half year. Duane blowing it all on lap dances and top-shelf liquor.

He slips down the stairs, careful of the squeaky fourth step, and retrieves the guitar. A few chord progressions, strummed soft. "Twin castles in the night," he sings, his voice slipping unconsciously into Gene's aggressive growl. But no, this wouldn't be a Gene song. This would be something different. Something totally his own. Fingering the chords again. "Twin castles twinkling bright," he sings, softer now, his real singing voice scratchy and high. "Twin castles..." What rhymes with bright? All right? He lets his fingers move along the frets. Pretty chords. With a little echo, some depth, a bass line underneath, it would sound okay. "Twin castles..." What? A few more chord changes. Then his fingers are moving along the frets, fingering the bass line from "Rock and Roll All Nite." Jesus, that feels good. "You show us everything you got," he growls. "Keep on dancin' and the room gets hot. You drive us wild

7

we'll drive you crazy."

Twin castles. Bullshit. Be Gene.

The address in the matchbook is only about ten minutes away. The kind of neighborhood you drive through on your way to another place.

He puts the guitar back in the case and walks upstairs. Into the bathroom. The cold cream container is half empty. Needs to make a new grocery list. He scoops an ice cream–sized ball of the stuff and smears it over the make-up, rubs in smaller and then larger circles, his eyes closed, until his entire face is covered. Then he reaches for the make-up towel and wipes slowly, away from his eyes, until all that's left is a dull residue. He splashes his face with water and rubs again with the other side of the towel. Outside, he hears thunder. He takes a tissue, removes a few specks of white or black, glances at himself, but not too long—not long enough—and steps back into the living room.

Fifteen minutes to meet Duane. It will take ten. He puts on his sneakers and opens the door, closes it without a sound.

THE JERRY GARCIA FINGER

EVERYTHING WAS GOING TO SHIT. I needed a change.
I decided to buy a car.

The lot was called Super Cars Deluxe, one of those
off-brand concrete fields, on a bad strip of highway dotted
with gas stations and check-cashing places and those joints
that sell carryout Chinese and subs and shrimp by the
pound and whatever else you might want a whole lot of
cheap. I wandered around what they were passing off as a
showroom, a shack just a little bigger than my apartment
with duct-taped windows and a vintage Dodge Charger
up on blocks in the middle, rust dripping into a pile under
the left fender.

A blonde with a black eye and make-up that looked like
it had been applied the night before sat behind a beat-up
desk. "Can I help you?" she said.

"Looking for a car," I said. "Something, you know,
badass."

"Levon," she said, and pointed out toward the lot and a
skinny guy in a bad suit.

"Looking for a car," I said to him. "Something cool." I
flashed on Candy packing up her gym bag, her tackle box

full of make-up and little brushes and mirrors and stuff I didn't even know what it was, the way her ass looked heading out the door.

Levon ran a hand through a pompadour, wiped it on his suit leg, shook my bad hand but didn't seem to notice. "Levon," he said. His hands were red and scaly, with white patches where it was flaking off. A few pieces slipped onto my hand and I wiped it on my jeans. He started walking. "Something cool, huh?" He was short and older than he should have been for working at a place like Super Cars Deluxe: wrinkles pulled tight on his face, a long nose with a drinker's red tip, a bushy mustache that was just starting go wild, a smell of Jägermeister that was so strong my mouth watered a little at first, and then I dry-heaved a little, and then my mouth watered again and I thought about stopping by Stubbie's on the way back home.

I took out a cigarette, considered it, and then put it back in the pack. "Something badass," I said.

"Got a trade-in?" he asked. He shook my hand again and I got confused wondering whether I made up the first handshake or he had already forgotten about it. "Do. You. Got. A trade-in?" Levon said again, louder, holding a scaly hand up to his ear like we were both hard of hearing.

He looked back to the office, where the blonde was knitting something. I waited him out. "Fuck it," he said. He leaned in close, his mouth only an inch or so from my ear. "You wanna get out of here, go chase some pussy?"

"What?" I said. I looked around at the beat-up cars, the chain-link fence blocking us off from some kind of factory chugging gray smoke.

"Pussy," he said. "Poooontaaaaang." He drew it out like he was talking about the best food you could ever eat.

"Women?" I asked.

"You betcha," he said. He grabbed my bicep and squeezed. He poked me in the belly. "Now he's catching on," he said, like it was a punch line, like there was some other guy there to hear it.

In my pocket, I was still carrying around the note from last week, the one that said, "You cheap bastard. See you around. Candy." I crumpled it inside of my fist. "Yeah, I think I do," I said.

"Well, let's us not fuck around, then," he said. "Let me show you the baddest motherfucker we have on the lot."

Me and Levon drove my new Charger out Route 11 toward Tiffany's Playpen. The clutch was slippery and the engine had a knock started up whenever we got over thirty, but he was right about it being badass. It was just about the most badass car I'd ever seen—Detroit steel, blue over white, 375 horses on a 440 block.

"Where you from?" Levon shouted. There was an air pocket in the left door and it sounded like we were racing a diesel engine neck and neck, even though we were inside my badass new Charger, listening to Boston on the classic rock radio. "Where you from?" Levon asked again. He did the hard of hearing thing with his ear, only this time I don't think he was joking.

"I'm from right here. Altoona," I said. The strip malls were getting fewer and farther between, opening up to little stands of woods or office buildings where people did I don't know what. Levon was looking at me and kind of tapping his hands, like he was Alex Trebek and my time was running out to answer the double jeopardy. "Oh yeah," I said. "So where you from?" This was happening to me a lot lately, ever since the accident: people waiting for me to hold up my end of a conversation. It was like I needed my oil changed, like my air filters were stuffed and anything that came in just got stuck there, smog hovering around inside my head, and no matter how much shit I bought or movies I watched, it all stayed the same.

"I'm from all over, my friend," Levon said. He waved his scaly hands to indicate the whole interior of the car. "Been all around this world." He said it like he was used to saying it, like this was one of his regular things to say, and I got the feeling I was going to hear it again a few times, like he was going to start telling me a story that would last all night, or maybe a few nights if I was drunk enough and our money didn't run out. But I didn't really care. I was happy enough to be moving in my badass car with this jumpy guy, heading toward a place where naked women would act like your friend as long as you kept buying drinks.

"Let's play a game," Levon said. He sucked from a little flask, burped Jäger smell into the Charger. "Paper, rock, scissors."

"I'm driving," I said.

"It's a kids' game," he said.

I considered this. It was a reasonable argument. Plus, my hands were starting to shake, and even secondhand, that Jäger smelled pretty good.

"So here's how it works," he said.

"I know how it works."

"We're gonna go one," he shook his fist, "two," another shake, "three," he shook again, "and then we throw. Got it?"

I held the wheel with my right so I could throw with my left, the one that still had all the proper digits. We were about ten minutes away, heading down Route 11 past the plant where I used to work until about a year ago.

"You understand?" he said. "We throw paper, rock, or scissors. None of this lizard or gun or fucking yoda bullshit."

"I'm waiting," I said, and I wiggled the fingers on my good hand, like they were getting impatient.

"One," we both shook our fists accordingly, "two... three...shoot!" Levon yelled.

I threw paper. He threw rock.

"Hah!" I said.

Levon took a shot from the flask and handed it to me. "Big winner," I said, and I took a snort. The liquor bit at first, then the barky licorice flavor took over and I could feel the warm moving down into my gut. My watery eyes felt right and the churn in my belly seemed like a lurch in the right direction.

"Double or nothing," he said. I threw rock to his scissors. "I'm homing in," he said, "figuring you out. I'm getting inside your head, jack." He slurped from the bottle and passed it over. I did the same and the feeling was slightly better this time. Things were definitely heading in a direction.

"Hey," I said. "Don't we have papers to sign or something? On the car, I mean."

He considered this for a second. "What do you have to put down?"

"I wasn't exactly sure about buying," I said, feeling my wallet, fat like a mousetrap in my pocket. "Something like two hundred, three hundred bucks," I lied.

"That'll do for now," he said. "Rest of it, we'll settle up on tomorrow."

"That doesn't sound quite right," I said. "Legal, I mean."

"Here," he said. "Let's seal her with a kiss." He held the bottle up to my mouth and I drank. "There we go," he said, like we had just merged our Internet companies and now it was just up to the lawyers to sign all the proper papers and mail them to our accountants.

Levon walked into Tiffany's like he owned the place. He called everybody by some kind of name but not the one they used normally—*Hey, man! Yo, chief! There he is! Hiya, captain! How's it hanging, guy? Howdy, friend!* I got the feeling like nobody liked him much, but they didn't want to take time out from the titties to make much about it. We settled in at the bar and he ordered a pitcher of Miller and two Jägers back. I didn't complain, even though it almost felt like we were on some kind of strip club date, just knocked back half a glass and the shot, then watched a skinny blond girl with black eyebrows shimmy out of a Walmart corset. I knew it was from Walmart because I bought the same one for Candy for Valentine's Day, and she just made a face like I was an asshole and asked if there was a gift receipt.

"The fuck happened to your hand?" Levon said.

I held up my right hand, let him look at it close. Half of the middle finger was missing. "Lost it in brake press out at Snyders. The sheet metal factory," I said. "Best day of my life, if you want to know the truth."

"Disability," he said.

"Settlement. Keep-my-mouth-shut money."

"Hit the fucking lottery," he said. "Lucky sonofabitch."

Truth was I had been trying to figure out what to do. I had been doing pretty much whatever I wanted for the past year—drinking good liquor, eating carryout, watching TV and old detective movies. I bought a boat and drove it a few times and then kind of forgot about it. A Jet Ski. A Fender Stratocaster that was played once by somebody in some band I never even really knew. But the money was running out and the badass Charger would pretty much take care of what I had left.

The blonde left the stage and a black girl with a nice body and hair pulled into a bun came jogging out. She was dressed like she was leading an aerobics class, sports bra and those tight shorts. "Here we go," Levon said.

"Let's Get Physical" came on and she started doing some kind of porno exercise routine, jumping jacks and then a trip up and down the pole, sit-ups, and then the sports bra landed on Levon's head, a few girl pushups and then the little shorts were sitting next to the sports bra. "Let's have that four hundred," Levon said, snapping his fingers at me. He kept his eyes on the girl. She was doing ab crunches, mixing in some deep lunges, and it took me a few seconds to realize he was talking to me.

"What?" I said.

"The down payment on the badass motherfucking Charger," he said.

"You mean the two hundred?"

"Fucking cheapskates," Levon said like he was used to it, like this happened all the time. For just a second, he took his eyes off the exercise lady and put them on me.

"You said two hundred," I said. I reached in my wallet and counted out ten twenties, laid them on the table. "This better be fucking legal," I said. I still had my hand over the money.

"Jesus," Levon said. "They really did a number on that finger, didn't they?"

"Brake press don't play around," I said, and stuffed my hand under my leg.

Levon moved the money over in front of him. The stripper was just doing normal stripper stuff now, moving around picking up dollars with her ass cheeks, although it did seem like she was flexing them a little more than she had to, and I had to admit that all those lunges looked to be paying off pretty good. Levon put a twenty in front of him and she picked it up real slow and blew him a kiss. Then she did a cartwheel and skipped back behind the little curtain.

"Fuck but she's a sight," Levon said. He wiped his brow with a cocktail napkin and signaled the bartender for another round.

"You sure that's legal?" I said.

"She damn well shouldn't be, friend," Levon said. "But I can assure you that Olympia is all of thirty-two years old."

"I mean the car. The down payment."

"Some people," he said. He slid a shot of Jäger in front of me like that would answer my question. I did the shot and tried not to think too much about paperwork or a title or insurance or any other stuff a cop might ask about.

"Let's play another," I said, holding out my fist. We counted it down and I threw rock to his scissors. "I believe I'm in your kitchen, my friend," I said, realizing that I was starting to talk like Levon and it was a little early to be feeling this good. I put it out of my mind and held my hand up in a fist.

We were about ten shots in, a full pitcher in front of us and Olympia the exercise stripper sitting between us, drinking twenty-dollar glasses of champagne Levon paid for right out of my down payment money, when Candy walked in. At that point I wasn't even surprised. I was more like, of course. I was like, maybe this is a good thing. I was like, if Candy wants to watch a girl do jumping jacks and then throw her sports bra and her little exercise shorts onto Levon's head, who am I to stop her? I didn't even think about who might be coming in behind her until I saw the biker.

He was the kind of fat that just looks thick. Both arms were full-sleeve tattooed and he wore his hair in a ponytail. He had a long beard but a teddy bear kind of face, like he could have been a top chef or an outlaw and decided on the one that got his ass kicked less but was still a little not sure about it.

He high-fived his way past the bouncer and the bartender and gave Levon a big pat on the back before he noticed Candy still tippy-toeing around by the door. "What the fuck?" he said. She waved him over and they had a little powwow and he turned and came right for me. "This is the gimp?" he said.

"Hey, friend," Levon said. "Nobody here has any quarrel with you." He looked at me like I was supposed to be doing something and I nodded.

"I'm not a gimp," I said.

"I thought you got, like, injured. Fucked up in some kind of accident or whatever," he said. I could smell the booze on him and he was already slurry. He nodded over to Candy teetering on the edge of the bar. I held up my hand to show him where the rest of my finger used to be.

"Holy shit," he said. He pulled up a barstool and grabbed my hand in his paw. I yanked but he was as strong as he looked. "Holy fucking shit." He ran a finger along my stump and I jumped. Nobody outside a doctor's office had done that yet, not even Candy, not even right after, when we were still going good, before she got moody and mean and interested in common-law marriage and joint accounts, IRAs and 401ks and exchange-traded funds. "You have it," he said. He looked at me like he was telling me my grandma's dogs playing poker painting was done by Picasso. "You have the Garcia finger. The Jerry Garcia finger. The exact fucking thing."

Levon and Olympia leaned over to get a better look. Candy was getting a drink at the bar. The dancer who was on stage, a hard brunette whom I had seen around a little, always pushing a whole passel of kids, had stopped dancing and was just standing there with her bra half off, trying to figure out what was happening.

"Hey," I said. And then, "Hey!" I yanked my hand out of his grip.

The biker held out his hand to shake, but it seemed like maybe it was a trick to get at my Garcia finger, whatever the hell that was, so I kept my right hand in my lap and reached out with my left. "Augustus," he said. "Augustus Reilly. That's the damndest thing I believe I've ever seen." He took off his jacket and rolled up his shirt, pointed at a tattoo of a skull with roses around it.

"Pretty," I said.

"You're not following," he said. He noticed Candy still hovering near the door. "Jesus Christ, Candy, get over here. The guy wouldn't harm a fucking fly, even you told me that."

I was wondering what Candy had told him and when, why the bartender knew to put a few limes in her Miller Lite draft, thinking a whole lot of shit was starting to make a whole lot of sense. Levon and Olympia had lost interest, safe in knowing the biker wasn't going to open any whoop-ass cans, at least not right now, not on me and my special Jerry Garcia finger, and she was demonstrating the deep knee lunges, talking about how you have to hold your midsection tight and not put a lot of strain on your back. Levon handed her another one of my twenties.

Candy had finished her beer and was sloshing the limes around in her glass and kind of standing behind Augustus. "You're the cheapest motherfucker I ever fucking saw in my whole fucking life!" she said. "There! I said it."

"What are you talking about?" I said. Levon laughed like he had figured out some kind of secret, and handed one more of my down payment twenties to Olympia, this time not even for doing anything at all.

"Win fifty thousand dollars and you don't even give a dime to your wife."

"My wife?"

"Common-law," she said. She drank the lime beer slush in her glass and waved the empty at the bartender. "Coulda been."

"Let me see that again," Augustus said. "That Jerry Garcia finger." He grabbed at my hand and I let him take it.

"I deserve something," Candy said.

Levon nodded his head like he agreed.

"And I didn't win nothing," I said. "I got fucking mutilated. And was given a settlement for my pain and suffering."

I tried to show her my stump but Augustus was running his hand along it again. "Amazing," he said. "Hey, you play any guitar?"

"You could say I paid pretty goddamn dearly for that fifty thousand," I said. "And anyway, the last of it is sitting right over there, most of it inside that sports bra, if you want to know the truth." I nodded at Olympia and she made a muscle.

"Asshole pisses away all his winnings on boats and fucking Blu-rays of old detective movies and doesn't share a red cent."

"You didn't go to Vegas, then?" I said. "You never got so drunk on that boat that I spent all day cleaning it out and it still smells like puke? You never rode on that Jet Ski?"

"Buys me a Valentine's day from Walmart," she said.

"Shut the fuck up," Augustus said. He said it firm but quiet, the way the head detective does in one of those old movies, where everybody is arguing and then all the sudden they're quiet because whatever this guy says is how things are gonna be. "Everybody shut the fuck up. I don't give a shit. This is fucking important." He let my fingers go and held out his arms in a way that said I should look at his tattoos. I noticed dancing bears and skulls and skeletons all lined up like Broadway. He pointed at one on the inside of his elbow. It was a hand just like mine, the middle finger just half there.

"You got a gift, son," he said. "My question is: what the fuck are you gonna do with it?"

"Piss it away on fucking Humphrey Bogart movies," Candy said. "Rifles and golf clubs and a drum set. A three-wheeler he's never even fucking sat on."

"I'm not even talking about that," Augustus said. "I'm talking about this Jerry Garcia finger." He wagged at my stump like it was a lottery ticket.

"I bought a car," I said.

"A beauty!" Levon said.

Candy harrumphed.

"A fucking car," Augustus said. He pulled his barstool even closer, took my hand like he was going to propose. "With great luck comes great responsibility," he said. "Spiderman said that. Or his grandma. We all seen that movie. Anyways, truer-ass words never been spoken." He was talking in that flat and soft detective way and everybody had stopped, was looking over at us like I was a high school running back about to announce whether it was Penn State or USC. "And let's face it, friend," he said. "You got fucking lucky."

"Fifty fucking grand," Candy said.

"I'm not talking about the fucking money!" he said. "I'm talking about his finger looks exactly like the one from the greatest guitar player ever. I'm talking about something would outlive each and every one of us in this bar, longer'n fifty thousand dollars would get each of us." He looked up at the ceiling like maybe whatever he was going to say next was too important to be saying in front of a bunch of jackasses like us, then he looked me right in the eye. "I'm talking about music. Taking that gift of yours and make some music with it."

"Let's Get Physical" came on the sound system again and Olympia jumped up and jogged toward the stage. "Jesus Christ," Augustus said, shaking his head like the song had disappointed him. "Well?" he said.

"What?" I said.

"What are you gonna do?"

I was getting sick of all the attention by now, sick of Candy with her remarks, this biker teddy bear and everything he wanted from my Jerry Garcia finger, of

Levon and the way he kept handing my money off to exercise strippers, sometimes just for sitting there in a sports bra.

I shook his hand and let him get a good rub at my Jerry Garcia finger. I stood up, saluted Levon like he was some kind of sailor captain, and walked out the door.

I was surprised to see it was night. We had been in that place for a long time, too long. It was cool but in the good way, like when you realize you've been too hot and all of the sudden you're not anymore. I saw the badass Charger sitting off to the side, and even with the paint peeling a little and me knowing that it was going to ping every time I got it up over thirty, and not really being sure whether I had even purchased it, I was happy to have the keys in my pocket.

I knew they had followed me out and was hoping it was just so Levon could show off the badass Charger, maybe get the biker interested in some Detroit muscle of his own. I guess I knew that was unlikely, even then, but with everybody telling me how lucky I was maybe I had got to believing it myself.

The first punch was somewhere around my ear and after that things went blurry and soft. The next couple were businesslike, and I knew the biker was just finishing up the deal and then the kicks were probably from the others. I could hear Candy yelling all kinds of crazy shit about Jet Skis and three-wheelers and the Cabela's catalog, and Levon breathing heavy and muttering fuck each time he kicked. I could hear the Harley start up and spray gravel, then the Charger turning over. I rolled over onto my back and heard the music hum of the strip bar and car wheels moving out toward the road. I saw the full moon and the stars like sparklers. I looked at my Jerry Garcia finger, that little stump that couldn't even say fuck you anymore, and I wondered if it was true that I was lucky.

ROCKABYE

Episode 1:

We see Daddy on Sundays at lunch. Sometimes Wednesdays, too, from eight until nine, if Mommy lets us watch the reruns.

This season it's harder to get her to let us watch. Last time, Mommy didn't care. For a while, she even thought it was funny. In the first episode, when Daddy came walking out with his new hair and his eyes with make-up like the TV ladies, Mommy yelled "Ohmygod" and almost spilled her wine and then called Aunt Lisa and shouted into the phone so much I almost couldn't hear Daddy explaining how he was looking for his real, one and only Rockin' Rockabye Baby and how he'd have to send one sexy lady home each week, and how this time he really wanted to find love.

Mommy thought that was the funniest part of all.

This year, Mommy says no way are we watching. "Why would you want to watch that?" she says.

"It's Daddy," I say.

She makes that huffy sound like she thinks something is funny but really she doesn't. "You're not old enough to watch this stuff," she says.

"Old enough like Sixx?" I say, and without trying I look toward my brother's room.

"I shouldn't have let you guys watch last year," she says, looking at Sixx's door and then down at the floor.

"It's Daddy," I say.

Mommy makes the funny noise again, shakes her head and lights a cigarette right in the house. But she lets me watch.

Later that night, when she thinks I'm sleeping, I can hear Mommy watching Daddy in the living room.

Episode 2:

Daddy calls and says he can't talk long because he's on a media tour but not like the tours he used to go on where they were all on a bus. A media tour is you talk to a whole bunch of people in a row, he says, but you stay in one place. It makes you tired.

"Mommy isn't here," I say.

"Good," he says. "I want to talk to you. Are you watching the show?"

I say yes but that Mommy doesn't like it much. Daddy says Mommy should be grateful that he had a few songs in him in the first place, and especially "Rockin' Rockabye Baby," which still brings in money and enough to buy the townhouse which is nice and a lot nicer than a tour bus or some of the places Daddy slept in between the last album and when the TV show started.

Daddy says we should pay attention to what Mommy says anyway, even if she is a...Daddy doesn't say what Mommy is.

"Can we come see you in California?" I say.

Daddy says he'll be back on tour in a few months and he'll see us after they play Baltimore. Daddy says soon we can come visit him in California, but not now, because he's still working some things out.

I say I got an A on my history project. "It was a report about Ben Franklin. Ben Franklin was…"

Daddy says he has to get going. "Sixx ain't there, is he?"

"Sixx is still out. Away."

"Gettin' his rocks off," Daddy says, and he laughs and sighs at the same time, and I can picture him shaking his head and kind of smiling, and he doesn't sound like he's mad at all.

Episode 3:

"Why don't you go play with your friends," Mommy says. "Play outside. Not watch TV all the time. Not *this* show."

"With who?" I say. "Outside where?"

Mommy nods. She turns on the TV. "Okay," she says.

Episode 4:

The girls on Daddy's show are pretty—shiny, with little dolly clothes and lots of colors on their cheeks and red happy lips that only get sad when Daddy tells them they have to go home now. They have fancy names like Lipstick and Gigi and Joey and Reb and Bikergirl, or place names like Memphis and Florida, or nice names like Sarah and Joanie and Cindy Lou.

I sit on the couch and Mommy sits back at the kitchen table. She acts like she's reading the newspaper but she has her glasses on and every now and then she huffs or laughs or whispers "Jesus" so I can tell she's watching, at least a little bit.

There's one girl, Dee, who looks just like Mommy but younger, Mommy in the pictures she hides in her desk. Dee used to have brown hair and then they dye it blonde on the fourth episode and when Daddy sees Blonde Dee he stops and makes a funny face and says "what's-a-goin'-on?" like he used to say to me when I was little, and he talks to somebody who isn't on the TV but off to the side. "Are you—*they bleep it out*—me?" he says. "You know what I'm talking about. She looks just like her."

"Mommy!" I say.

Mommy gets up and leaves.

Episode 5:

On Sunday at lunch I sit down to watch the show and Mommy says we're going to the movies.

"I don't want to go to the movies," I say.

"We're going to the movies," she says. Mommy looks tired. She's been driving around looking for Sixx a lot, calling his phone, sending email and stuff. At night, sometimes she gets really sad.

"Daddy's on," I say.

"Baby," Mommy says, "I have to go to the movies. I have to get out of here."

"But Daddy."

Mommy looks out the window. A boy rides by on his bike and Mommy watches him go. "Ozzy, can we please?" she says. Her voice is funny and she sits down, keeps on looking out the window even though the boy is gone. The sun is shining in her eyes and she's looking outside but not really looking at anything. There are little lines around her eyes, little hairs under her nose, soft, like the ones Sixx tried to turn into a mustache but it never worked, not yet anyway, not last time he came home to fight with Mommy. "Come on," she says. "To the movies."

The red light is on. Daddy is recording.

"Okay," I say.

Episode 6:

Sixx comes home right in the middle of the ceremony, when Daddy is deciding between the big girl with the funny accent or the little one with the blue hair. "I have two sexy ladies," he says, "and only one gold record left." He holds the record necklace thingy that he gives to the ladies he wants to stay. The camera moves to Dee. She gets the first gold record almost all the time now. Her hair is pulled back and she looks worried and she looks more like Mommy than ever.

Sixx just walks in like he's been here all along, slaps me on the back of the head, and opens up the refrigerator, drinks milk straight from the carton. He smells funny, sweet and smoky like one of Daddy's concerts. His hair is longer and the mustache is kind of coming in. "What's up, douchebag?" he says.

From upstairs, Mommy yells, "Who's that?"

Sixx gives me the look and I shut my mouth.

"Who's there!" Mommy yells, but it's not a question anymore, and she runs down the stairs and hugs Sixx real long and hard. I turn the TV off even though Daddy hasn't made his decision yet.

Mommy pulls back. "Where the hell have you been?" she says.

"I been around," Sixx says. I can tell he's trying to say it cool, like Daddy, but it comes out kind of whiny, like the funny guy on the show about high school.

"So what are you doing?" Mommy says. "Are you dropping out of school now? Running away from home? Seriously, what are you doing?"

"We're starting a band," Sixx says.

Mommy gets real quiet. She looks like she's thinking. "A band," she says.

Sixx nods.

"A band." She smiles, laughs, gets that look like she's not looking at anything. "Get up to your room," she says. "You are as grounded as anybody has ever been. You are the world record in grounded."

"No," Sixx says.

"Yes."

"*He* didn't," Sixx says.

"What do you mean, he didn't?"

"I mean him. Dad. He didn't listen to you or Grandma or anybody who wanted to crush his dreams."

"Oh God," Mommy says.

I'm wishing I kept the TV on. On TV the arguing is funny. Girls crying over Daddy, yelling at each other that they're not really there for Daddy, getting all red in the face and funny-looking and sometimes even throwing up or falling down. But here, Sixx and Mommy, this isn't funny. I push into the couch, let my stomach go flat, slip down into the cushion. I know about chameleons and I wish I could turn my whole body couch green and just slip back upstairs and see who did Daddy send home, what's gonna happen next week.

"I hate to tell you this, sweetheart, but you're probably old enough to know," Mommy says. She puts a hand on Sixx's arm. "Your father is an asshole."

Sixx nods. He opens the cupboard and takes a whole thing of cookies and a bag of pretzels. He walks out the front door and a car starts up and they drive off.

"Daddy's a what?" I say. I don't want to cry but I can feel it starting up.

Mommy picks up the phone and then she puts it back down again. "Shit," she says.

Episode 7:

I get sick for a whole week, a week I stay in bed. I'm hot and then cold and then sitting on the toilet. Mommy takes my temperature and calls the doctor and has to stay home from work. Mommy says, "It's okay, baby." She sings the slow song from Daddy's first album and it sounds even better than Daddy. Her voice is scratchy and sad like I feel, and I wonder if Sixx is ever going to come home again, and I don't even think about who Daddy chose and if they made Dee look even more like Mommy.

Episode 8:

Today, for the first time, one of the girls has a sleepover with Daddy. It's not Dee, but the other one Daddy likes, the one who wears her bathing suit all day and likes to climb onto Daddy and kiss him at dinner. She leaves Daddy's room wrapped in a blanket and the rest of the girls call her names.

Mommy takes the big picture of Daddy and the band and their first gold record, the one for "Rockin' Rockabye Baby," off the kitchen wall and puts it in the closet. "Too much," she says. "Too much."

The next day when I go downstairs to eat my cereal, it's back up again.

Episode 9:

Sixx hasn't been home since Daddy picked the girl with the blue hair instead of the big one with the funny accent. Mommy says he's going to wind up in jail. Mommy says Sixx is a chip off the old block, then she makes that funny not-funny sound and pours more wine.

Daddy calls and talks to me on the speakerphone. Mommy tells him I have to go. Daddy asks if Sixx is still getting his rocks off. Mommy says Sixx is just a kid and it's not funny. Daddy says a chip off the old block.

Episode 10:

Daddy makes the girls play basketball and they're all terrible at it except the girl named Dee, the one who looks like Mommy. Dee scores all the points and goes on a date with Daddy. She gets the logo for his band tattooed on the back of her neck.

Mommy can't believe this. She has three glasses of wine and two cigarettes, right in the house. She calls Aunt Lisa on the phone. "Are you watching this?" She says. "Turn on VH1. He's on there. No, no," she says. "This chick. I know! Wait, wait. Look at what she's doing!"

I hear Aunt Lisa laughing through the phone, all the way from Philadelphia.

"Hey, I might have these two," Mommy says, and she looks at the phone but I know she's talking about me and Sixx, "but at least I never did that."

Episode 11:

There are only three ladies left on Daddy's show and he spends most of the time going out on dates with each one. Mommy sits down with a glass of wine and a cigarette. She watches Daddy and the little girl with the blue hair dancing. Daddy spins her and then does a little jig thing that he does on stage sometimes.

"He always was a good dancer, your father," Mommy says.

"Really?" I say. She hasn't talked about Daddy like this for a long time. She nods, sips her wine.

Daddy kisses the blue-haired girl and Mommy sighs. "How old do you think she is?" she says. She picks up the phone and I know she's dialing Aunt Lisa's number.

"Maybe as old as you?" I say.

"You think that's how old I am?" Mommy says.

"But not as pretty as you," I say.

She puts the phone down. "You're a good boy," she says.

Episode 12:

I get pulled out of school on Friday and Mommy is waiting in the office. She doesn't say anything, just starts walking real fast, and I follow. We drive to the hospital and pick up Sixx, who they wheel out in a wheelchair, but he isn't even joking around, just kind of looking off to the side like he's embarrassed. "Hey, douchebag," I say, and Mommy punches me in the arm. Sixx doesn't even give a comeback.

He stays in his room for two days. Mommy goes in and comes out. Daddy calls and just talks to Mommy, talks to Sixx, but not me. I want to ask him who he's going to choose for his final Rockabye Baby. I want to say I was sick but I'm better now. But I know now isn't the time.

Finally, Sixx comes out on Sunday lunch and he heats up some soup, sits down on the couch. They cut his hair and shaved his almost mustache and he looks like Sixx again, just normal Sixx who used to play Risk and fantasy football and travel team soccer.

"How's this been?" he says.

"There's a lady who looks just like Mommy," I say. "Daddy might choose her."

"That I doubt," he says.

We watch Daddy on his dates and we eat soup. "He told me who he picks," Sixx says. I look at him quick and he smiles. "Nah, he didn't," he says. I'm not so sure, but I sit back and try not to think about Daddy telling Sixx who his Rockabye Baby is when he didn't even want to talk to me.

Mommy comes downstairs and makes a cup of tea for her and one for Sixx. She makes me hot chocolate and we all watch Daddy and the two girls. Daddy is wearing a tie and a T-shirt, with messy jeans and a top hat. His hair is long and yellow and Mommy shakes her head and sighs.

They show a close-up of Dee. "Oh my god," Sixx says. "Mom, that girl looks just like you when you…"

"I know," she says. "Let's hope he doesn't make the same mistake twice."

They both laugh and I look at them to see what was funny but they just watch the show and it feels nice to be sitting there with Sixx and Mommy again and even if I'm not sure what they're talking about, at least Sixx is here and they're not yelling.

We all sit there for a minute while Daddy hands the last gold record to the other girl, the one with the blue hair. "Will you be my Rockabye Baby?" he says, and he's crying a little bit. The blue girl cries too, and nods and nods and nods. Daddy hugs her and they both cry while the other girl, the one who looks like Mommy, starts yelling at everybody.

She starts slow, then gets a little louder, then she gets really mad and they have to bleep out most of what she's saying and what everybody is saying back to her. She throws something and something breaks. Daddy is backing up. His hair comes off with his top hat and then he looks like Daddy used to and I say "Daddy!" and he grabs his hair and puts it back on again and pulls the blue-haired girl back and back and they trip over stuff and Dee keeps on yelling.

Mommy is laughing and Sixx is yelling, "Go, go, go." The screen goes black and we can hear more stuff crashing, Mommy and Sixx are both laughing and I am too and I don't know why, and when the show stops we all keep on doing it for a long time.

DEATH AND THE WIGGLES

OF ALL THE THINGS Sherri did not take with her when she ran away to Myrtle Beach with the dentist— the house and the car and the toddler, the drawer full of lingerie that I can't bear to throw away but also can't imagine keeping, and in what I have to admit are my darker times I find myself actually smelling; the clothes, pictures, Lean Cuisines, shampoo, body cleanser, soap, razors, and tampons—of all those left-behind things, the tickets to the Wiggles concert are the one thing I actually wish she would have taken. She bought them months ago, long before she dropped the news about the "emotional affair" with the dentist, which was followed shortly, of course, by the news about the physical affair with the dentist. "It's so intense," her note said. "I owe it to myself to explore this." And then, like the Magellen of late-thirties sexuality, she was gone.

So now here I am, in the pizza line at the Bryce Jordan Center, where Penn State plays basketball, with Ian's head pushed against my knees and Woomer pouring Beam into his thirty-two-ounce diet cola while pudgy housewives in garish sweatpants and Sansabelt jeans shuttle two or three or, Jesus, four kids through the lines that snake up and down the concourse.

There's a vibe in the air but it's nothing like any concert I've ever attended. These kids know something is happening, but they have no idea what. The arena has been transformed. The last time I was here was to see the Zac Brown Band, semi-hippies lounging everywhere, the whole place smelling like clove cigarettes and weed and sweat. Now, toddlers. Mommies and daddies pulling along strings of crying or confused children, nursery school music pumping innocuously into the air. A strong scent of popcorn and dirty diapers.

"Pepperoni?" I ask Ian. He nods, still holding my hand, confused and clearly overwhelmed.

"Me too," says Woomer.

"That wasn't part of your deal," I say.

There are some times when I just can't manage this toddler stuff alone, and this is one of them. In exchange for his "support," I've agreed to pay Woomer's bar tab at Brownie's for a month.

"Dude," he says. "Look around. I think it might be time to renegotiate."

"Just be cool," I say.

"Be cool?" Woomer says. "I *am* cool. I'm the only one in this crowd wearing jeans that were purchased in this decade." He waves his hands at the crowd, almost clips a pudgy woman with twins in matching overalls. "Do you have any idea how far from cool we are right now?"

"Yeah," I whisper, aiming my voice away from Ian, careful to look around for anybody I might recognize.

This is a small town—small enough that no more than two days after Sherri left with the dentist I could already see the pity in the teachers' eyes when I dropped Ian off at preschool. "Actually, I do."

Woomer pulls out his flask and pours more into his Coke.

"Aren't you at least a little worried about seeing a client here tonight?" I say.

Woomer is a lawyer who has literally made a career out of defending drunks of all stripes. His ad on the local college radio station proclaims a litany of the things he is more than willing to defend: drunk driving, public urination, shoplifting, public drunkenness, underage drinking.

"My clients are unlikely to be at the Wiggles concert," he says. "The people who are actually here? They're the ones who are cursing my clients, who waited a few minutes longer before they left the house tonight, waiting for my clients to show up as promised and thinking holy fuck, he's not going to blow off little Jimmy for the fucking Wiggles, is he?"

"Excuse me?"

I turn around to see a woman who is probably my age but looks about twenty years older. She's wearing a Penn State sweat suit and has a Wiggles sticker affixed to each cheek. Attached to her are three children with matching stickers. She gives Woomer a look that is intended, I'm sure, to shame him into shutting his mouth, putting his flask away, pretty much ceasing to be Woomer.

Woomer looks her up and down, lingers on the bottom half. He takes a cigarette out of his pack and puts it, unlit, into his mouth.

She opens her eyes a little wider.

"The children?" she says.

"Sorry," he says. "I don't do pack-moochers."

"Okay!" she says, speaking to the children, to Woomer, to anybody within earshot. "Let's go, Ronny, Bobby, and Michelle! Since some people don't know how to behave in public! And some people have been drinking! And using no-no words! And are generally a-holes! We have to get our pizza somewhere else!" Her voice rises with every word, until she's screaming, yanking her distressed brood, who are now more interested in Woomer than ever, down the concourse.

"That was weird," Woomer says.

In the background, I hear music starting up—simple and inoffensive, it sounds like a far-off carnival. An Australian accent booms, "Ah you rehdy? Foh the Weegles?" The next sound is a high, confused screech, cheers mixed with cries.

"Oh no," Woomer says. His face has gone dark, as if he's only just now realized exactly what we are doing here.

I wonder how much he had to drink before we picked him up. Me, I stuck with beer, which is why I'm staring at his flask and wondering if there's enough in there to make this seem funny and not tragic.

It's not that we were unhappy. Or particularly happy. We were doing okay, I thought. Sure, I noticed she'd gotten distant, but it had been happening for so long, it was like a bad ankle that gets worse as you age. At what point do you decide that an operation will be less painful than living with the day-to-day?

We're herded down some stairs and through the tunnel where the basketball teams make their entrance. At the bottom, security personnel in yellow T-shirts are checking tickets. "Miss Summer!" Ian shouts.

"No, Ian," I say. "Miss Summer is at school. We're at the Wiggles now."

I flash on Miss Summer, the assistant in his preschool room. Eyes like Kate Beckinsale. Blond hair. Early twenties. Just enough curves. If Miss Summer were here, I think, I'm pretty sure I would notice.

"Miss Sum!" he says. "Miss Sum."

But then, sure enough, there she is in a yellow security T-shirt, taking tickets and pointing out seat numbers.

"Hi, Ian!" she says, seeming unsurprised to find us here. I realize she must have seen most of his class by now. We arrange ourselves around her—three men of varying ages and states of decay. She is dazzling, confounding, like a mermaid or a fairy princess suddenly appeared in our midst.

"Chuck Woomer!" Woomer says, extending a hand. She shakes. He extracts a business card and squeezes her arm, runs his palm halfway down her back. "You can never tell when you might need a friend," he says. "So please, do give me a call."

I've seen him do this little number maybe one hundred times over the past few years, but for some reason, it turns my stomach and I get a lump in my throat, pull Ian toward me and rub his head. I look around. Everywhere, doting parents and excited little kids. I shouldn't have convinced Woomer to come. At the time, it seemed like a lark, a gonzo outing we'd laugh about over beers. Now it just seems like another drunken misstep, a symptom of the thing that is wrong with me. Ian wants to be here, and that should be enough. It should be that simple.

Miss Summer puts the card in her pocket and turns to me. "How *are* you?" she says. "I'm so…we're all just so sorry about everything."

"I'm fine," I say. "Fine. Just…" I have no idea what to say. I'm fine except I always thought I would be the one to leave? Fine except for the fact that I masturbate nightly, baking in a whiskey sweat, while holding my ex-or-whatever wife's boyshorts up to my nose?

"Oh my god, I'm so sorry!" she says. For a second, I wonder if I've actually said all those things out loud. Miss Summer points behind us, where a line thirty deep is getting increasingly louder. This mixes with the sound of the concert, and it's as if we are caught between two warring factions of jolly elves. She looks at our tickets. "You have great seats!" she says. "Just head on up there to row twenty-two and you're right on the aisle."

When she left, I was so sure she would have taken Ian that I was halfway through a bottle of Beam, a half hour late to meet up with Woomer at Brownie's, when the preschool called.

"He's...what?" I said. The note hadn't mentioned Ian, but what kind of mother leaves town with a dentist and doesn't even bring her kid?

"He's here," Miss Mary said, her voice sharp as a slap. "We've been calling Sherri's cell phone for an hour now, and she's not answering. I do hope everything is okay?"

I had been calling Sherri's cell phone for about two hours, shouting "whore!" into it, which explained why she would have turned it off. "No," I said. "I mean, I'll be there in fifteen minutes."

We do have great seats: on the floor, not too close but not far away either. We're right on the aisle, which here, at the Wiggles, is a wide concourse with room for entranced toddlers to dance. The children have one of two reactions: numb confusion or full-on toddler spaz-out. Ian is of the first group, and stands on my lap, enraptured by the grown men who skip around the stage singing preschool songs and cavorting with a pirate and a green dinosaur.

I wasn't sure if this would actually be the Wiggles—the same four men who hypnotize my son each night before bed. But sure enough, here they are: Anthony, Sam, Jeff, and Murray, of the blue, yellow, purple, and red shirts. There it is: the big red car. There is Captain Feathersword with his eyepatch and sword made of feathers. There is Dorothy the Dinosaur and Henry the Octopus and the Wiggles Dancers.

Ian is entranced. He looks like he's on an acid trip: eyes and mouth agape, a completely open receptacle, absorbing all the information pouring in from the stage. If you've never been to a concert before, or don't even know what one is, it must be an astounding thing. The Wiggles—these men from the television, all of a sudden appearing here, in front of him, in the flesh? It is a total mindfuck.

There are times, like right now, when Ian looks so much like his mother that it makes me want to cry and then smash a television. I elbow Woomer, motion for the flask, knock down a few shots. Woomer finishes it up and stuffs the empty container back in his pocket. He takes a half-pint of Beam out of his jacket and offers it to me. He is sweating, his straggly hair hanging down, his bald spot shining in the concert lights.

"We need to go to Jazzfest this year," he shouts. "I swear to God, nothing better in the world. Music and booze. Food. Or Bonnaroo. You ever been to Mardi Gras, even?"

"Mardi Gras?" I say, motioning to Ian. "*Really?*"

Onstage, Anthony is talking about happy pirates. I rub Ian's head and point to the stage. "Look, buddy, it's Captain Feathersword." The pirate is hanging upside down from a cartoonish castle, coughing out his usual exclamations of oohs and ahs, aarghs, and hee hee hees.

Woomer looks left, looks right, then kneels down and starts pouring Beam into a crack in the floor covering. He rubs the liquor into the floor with his foot, then does it again.

"What are you doing?" I say.

"It's under there—the basketball floor," he says. "And there's like a big crack in this covering thing right here, under my chair. Lucky fucking break."

"What are you talking about?"

"Think about it. Next year we'll be sitting here watching the Nittany Lions getting their asses kicked by Michigan State and right there, like forty feet away from the hoop, there'll be this little spot, and we'll know."

"We'll know what?"

"That's my mark. Right there."

"Really? *That* is your mark?"

Woomer shrugs. "I might go see how your friend is doing. Miss...what was her name? Blonde?"

"Miss Summer," I say.

"Miss Summer!" he shouts. "Perfect." He laughs, too loud.

I think about Miss Summer. She is clean and beautiful and uncomplicated. She probably knows things about Ian that I don't, has recognized changes I don't want to see yet. I am willing to bet she pays her bills on time, never leaves dishes in the sink, doesn't call in to work hung over, would never drive drunk to buy more cigarettes while a young child is sleeping.

"Stay away from Miss Summer, man," I say. "She's a nice girl. She doesn't need to get involved in any of this."

"What the hell does that mean?" Woomer says. "I don't think I like the way that sounds."

"I'm serious," I say.

"Sometimes even I wish Sherri had stayed," Woomer says. I think it's supposed to be a joke, but I'm not sure, and neither one of us is laughing.

We've spoken exactly once since she left. "How is he?" she said.

"Are you fucking kidding?" I said.

"I did this as much for you as for me," she said.

What could I say to that? What could that mean? I just sat there, noticing how dirty the floor was and listening to the sound of Ian's sleep machine, white noise trickling through the monitor.

"I didn't think you'd be ready," she said. In the background, I heard smooth jazz and the tinkle of dishes being prepared. She hung up.

"Ian is all kinds of fucked up," I said, still holding the phone, shouting into it. "He needs a mother and his father drinks too much and hasn't read any of the parenting books and is all kinds of fucked up himself so how is anybody in this house supposed to..." I stopped, looked at the phone, considered smashing it on the dining-room table, grinding it into bits until my fingers were bloody, and then laid it carefully back in the receiver.

Anthony Wiggle, the one in the blue shirt, seems obsessed with doing headstands. Not handstands. Headstands. That's a handstand with a male dancer holding you around the waist. This guy is supposed to be some kind of role model for my three-year-old son?

Ian has made the transition from numb to toddler spaz-out, and he is dancing in my lap, jumping up and down, up and down, throwing his body around with the reckless abandon of a Deadhead spinner. The Wiggles sing, "Toot toot chugga chugga big red car, toot toot chugga chugga big red car," and his face is pure joy. This is as happy as he's been since Sherri left, as happy as I can ever imagine him being.

Ian is happier right now, I think, than I will ever be again in my entire life.

I think about the life of vague unhappiness and disappointment that he's got before him, endless numbered days, as they say. I watch him jump, his face, Sherri's face, the same sloe eyes and sandy hair, the same nose with its little indent on the tip, a beautiful imperfection. I place him on the floor and he bounces around the concrete.

"Hey, man," Woomer says. "I'm not feeling so great. I think I need a cigarette or something."

"You just want to go put your little act over on Miss Summer."

Onstage, Dorothy the Dinosaur is singing about her garden. The Wiggles skip around her in a ragged circle. Ian is dancing. It is the first time I have seen him really sweat.

"There's something almost sexual about what's happening up there," Woomer says, nodding at the stage. He stretches his arms, rubs at a spot on his back, and then he collapses.

Woomer is a big man, and when he goes down, he takes out half of our row. Folding chairs go flying, toddlers scamper. It's dark and nobody knows what is happening. People grab their children. Kids laugh and point, thinking that, on this magical night, when the Wiggles step out of the television and into Central Pennsylvania, anything out of the ordinary must be part of the act. I think at first that he's just had too much whiskey, but I've seen Woomer drink four times what he's had tonight, and I've never seen him pass out or even so much as slur his words. His breathing is shallow and his face is the color of hot dogs.

"Call 911!" I shout. And then Security is here. Miss Summer kneels down in her yellow shirt and puts an ear to Woomer's mouth. I almost expect him to whisper something dirty, slide his fat tongue into her lovely ear, but his eyes are rolled back in his head and I'm not even sure if he's breathing. Somewhere in there, I've grabbed Ian, and I'm clutching him to my chest. His head twitches back and forth between the Wiggles on stage and the floor, where Miss Summer is administering CPR. She alternates breathing into Woomer's mouth and pushing at his chest, stopping every now and then to listen for a heartbeat. She is bent over Woomer, her khaki pants riding down to reveal the slim line of her thong, pink and satiny. This woman teaches my son, she is maybe the most important female figure in his life right now, she is trying to save the life of my best friend, and all I can do is wonder at that thin strip of satin, stare at it and think about the implications: Miss Summer is wearing a thong.

The Wiggles are thanking us for a wonderful night and telling us to listen to our parents and to visit their website for more Wiggly fun. The house lights come up slowly and the EMTs show up, ask Miss Summer a few questions, then put Woomer on a stretcher and as quickly as it happened, he is gone. Everybody is filing out of the auditorium. Miss Summer is standing off to the side. A young man who looks like the leader of a band I'm not cool enough to know about has a hand around her waist, whispering into her ear. Ian is crying and I tell him everything will be okay. He smiles Sherri's smile and I know that he believes me, and that makes me wish more than anything that what I'm telling him is true.

POP STAR DEAD AT 22

DO YOU KNOW what it's like when Facebook tells you they have to pull your profile because you're getting too much traffic? When Justin Bieber follows you on Twitter? And then the next day, Miley Cyrus? I mean *they* are following *you*. You know that's like? I do, bro. It's fucking awesome.

And then all of the sudden, the bottom just drops out? Dude. One minute you're cruising down the street, waiting for a callback from the people at The Soup. The next, you're reading the headline on TMZ—Pop Star Dead at 22.

Now everything else is going to be after, and before is going to be the good times, like those '80s drug movies where everything is awesome and funny and bubbly soundtrack until somebody's nose starts bleeding, and then it's all rehab, narcs, and power ballads, everybody crying and getting too skinny and sad and ugly.

I remember before—that night when we were getting ready to go out and I was like, I don't know if I should wear the Calvin Klein boxer briefs or the Hugo Boss tighty-whiteys, and something in my gut said tighty-whitey, dude. And I didn't think much about it until way later, after her people came over and told us to go into the private room, and our crew is hanging with her crew and we're all looking at each other going, Dude, I can't believe this either, but trying to be cool about it, too, like this happens to us all the time. And she's like, Let's go skinny dipping! And I'm like, Sure! And later on, when we're by the pool, and I'm trying to catch a glimpse and her people are taking away my phone, she's all, I really like a man in tighty-whiteys. And I laughed and felt kind of like a tool, you know, because she is her and I'm like just some random dude at the bar, right? And she was like, Seriously, I really do.

That's how she was, though. Old fashioned. Honest. Like, I believe she really did like a dude in tight-whiteys, and not many chicks will tell you that and really mean it.

She was different.

People say they could see it coming and maybe that's the case if you weren't actually there. If you were, like, you know, so far away from her that you could sit up there in your glass tower and say, I, dude in glass tower, could totally see it happening: this pop star, who we all loved like the sexy girl-next-door you want to not just hook up with but maybe actually cunnilingate in a loving fashion, that's how clean and nice and wholesomely sexy she was, is heading for a Philip Seymour Hoffman and she's heading there fast.

People might say all we shared was that one night but they don't understand. They didn't really know her. Not like me. Like I told Perez, I don't kiss and tell, but let's just say that yes, we were intimate, and that yeah, there's a real good chance we were going to be in love.

Did you know that I texted her that night? She was pronounced at midnight, and I texted at like ten. I wonder if she got it, but there's no way I can know. I think about that a lot, whether it would have made a difference.

I picture her there, just before—maybe she's wearing a dress, kind of frilly, a little old fashioned, a little Southern, not the kind of thing that's going to ride up while she gets out of a limo. Maybe she's not wearing any make-up and yeah, maybe she has a few zits, like a real girl, but prettier. Her hair is still a little wet from the shower and she's sitting there in her hotel room, way up on top of the LA hills, and maybe she's thinking about me—that one guy, the normal one, tighty-whitey guy who went skinny dipping and made out and shared a few laughs, a Marlboro Menthol or two, the guy who maybe reminds her of all the guys back home who she never got a chance to date—the not bad guys, the ones who would have been normal and nice and treated her good, who maybe would have taken her out for an ice cream sundae, a trip to the movies, a real date.

I picture her there with her legs tucked under her, twirling a piece of hair and thinking about how did a nice girl like her even get into a place like this and does anybody understand at all, and maybe she's wondering what happened to that one guy who seemed like maybe he could, like maybe he did understand.

I wonder if she ever got my text. Here's something I never told anybody before—not even Buzzfeed. You don't even have to mention my name, not if you don't want to. That's how serious about I am about all this.

That last text, it said, "Howz it goin gurl?" So maybe that's what her last text said: Howz it goin, gurl? Think about that: her last text. That shit should be in the Smithsonian.

When I sent it, I meant so much more. I meant this means so much to me. I meant I have finally arrived. I meant every day of delivering pizzas and folding T-shirts and working out and trying new things with my hair until it was just fucking right was all worth it. I meant thank you.

I wonder if she got it. I wonder if she understood.

Anyway, like I said before, you can use it if you want to.

INTERLUDE:
COVER SONG

GOLIATH

WE ARE TRAPPED in the old silver mine again. Everything is black and cold. It is different but not unfamiliar
and I realize almost immediately that I am dreaming, that
I am in the episode again. Fifteen minutes, I think. All I
have to do is get through fifteen minutes. Soon, as always,
the temperature will become unbearable. I will get hungry,
desperate. My breath will grow short and the black void
will seem insurmountable. Although I can't see a thing,
I know we are hunkered beneath a beam. In front of us,
or behind, a mass of rock and dust from floor to ceiling.
I can't hear the heavy dog breath, his playful and sincere
voice, but I know that he is here, somewhere, waiting for
my call, my touch, waiting for me to give up, lose faith, to
reach the bottom of my capacity for belief. He is waiting so
he can teach me the lesson.

"Davey!" a voice calls.

I fumble for my line, but I can't remember a thing.
Again, this is the dream. In real life, I almost never forgot
a line. If we had to do more than two takes, it was almost
always his fault. Although I'm far removed from my acting

days, I could still recite most of the scripts verbatim, both of our parts, all five seasons.

"Daaaa-viiiiiid." Wait. This voice is different, not the usual dream, not his voice at all. A woman's voice. Now she is grunting, sighing. She whistles. Whistles? "Daaaa-viiiiiid," she sings.

I wake up with a start. Drool is plastered down my chin. I reach for my glasses.

"That took long enough," Sandy says. "The dream again, huh? The coal mine."

"Silver," I say.

"Like I said, I never really watched," she says. "No offense."

"None taken," I croak. And I really mean it. This is one of the things I love most about Sandy. Her parents were hippies who didn't own a television. Child star? She could care less.

She's dressed in her running stuff. The bedroom in the condo is little, and she barely has enough room for a hurdler's stretch between the bed and the TV. She stands, leans over and grabs her ankles, allows her head to fall almost down to her knees. The phone rings and she pops back up.

After three weeks, I still love watching these private moments, the arch of her back as she wipes sweat from her brow, leans over, and checks the caller ID. "Your mom," she says.

I hold my hand over the receiver and clear my throat. "Hey," I say, trying not to sound too hung over. How did last night end? Did we drink all our housewarming presents?

"You sound terrible," Mother says, her voice as clear as a church choir. "Shouldn't you be somewhere?"

"Late service."

Sandy rolls her eyes, leans over to stretch her calves.

"We need a favor," Mom says. "We're going on vacation and the dog sitter fell through. We need you to watch Goliath."

"When?"

"Next week."

Sandy is doing toe-touches. "I don't know, Mom."

"He'll only be staying a week, David. For goodness's sake, we thought you'd be excited about it."

"It's just, I don't know." How can I explain? She's never really understood what it was like between us. Not really.

"He's not what he used to be, I suppose," Mom says. "But I thought that after all your little adventures," she pauses and I can practically see the montage playing in her head—the soapbox derby, the time I fell through the ice at the old pond, the two of us trapped in the mine.

"After all our adventures what, Mom?" I wobble toward the living room. I smell coffee.

Sandy blows a kiss and heads out the door at a trot. I watch her bouncing gently down the street in her easy runner's gait. Sometimes I can't believe how lucky I am.

"I thought you'd be a little more sympathetic to an old friend, is all," Mother says.

"Look, Mom." How to say this? "He's not like ordinary dogs."

"I don't know what you're talking about, David."

Of course, I remind myself. She never did know—not really, not the full extent of it, what happened when the cameras were off. "Okay. We'll watch him."

"We?"

"I mean I'll watch him."

She pauses. Just long enough to let me know she knows something is off. She doesn't say anything, would never come out and actually *say* anything. This is the Lutheran way. "Fine," she says. "We'll be there Saturday morning. And it really would be nice to meet this *girlfriend* of yours."

"You are a freak," Sandy says. We're sitting on the little balcony, watching the traffic move back and forth on the highway. We're drinking Mexican beer and listening to Etta James. "I can't believe you still haven't told them we're living together."

"It's not that easy," I say. "He's...religious."

I swallow, try to hide how worried I really am. I've been dreading this day, when I can't hide it any longer. Sandy is beautiful, the best-looking woman I've ever spoken to, much less dated. More than that, she is cool. She knows the right bands and the right clothes and her friends look like extras from a beer commercial.

I am not cool. Thankfully, we're at an age when coolness is starting to matter less. She knows nothing of my embarrassing elementary school years, the awkward Christian middle school, the disaster of trying to fit into public school after the show got cancelled and Father lost the pharmacy. All she knows is that I am solid and reliable.

I express my feelings. I have a good job. I dress like a grown-up, I have a savings account, I am reserved enough to convey the spirit of still waters running deep.

"So are we just never going to tell your father, then? What about your mother?"

"That's not what I mean," I say. But of course I can't explain what I mean.

"I'm going to put up with this once," she says. "Next time your parents come down here, you go up there, you have to tell them."

I kiss her on the forehead.

"You're a freak," she says.

She has no idea.

"How do I look?" Sandy says. She's dressed in a long white skirt with a light blue tank top. Her hair is still wet.

"Perfect," I say. The doorbell rings and I jump.

"Calm down," Sandy says. She squeezes my arm, kisses me on the cheek. "It's just your parents."

My mother breezes through the door, followed by my father, and then Goliath. I'm surprised at how old my parents look. How long has it been? Since Easter. Six months. Mother is the Iggy Pop of elderly housewives, all stringy muscles, nervous energy, and silent judgment. She scans the apartment, looking for weaknesses, like a dog exploring the perimeter of a fence. She shakes Sandy's hand. My father waves hello and makes his way to the bathroom.

Goliath looks the same as ever, like a cross between a Great Dane and a Chesapeake Retriever, all head and elbows and the big grin he wears most of the time. He bounds behind my father, jumps on me and whimpers.

"Oh my god," Sandy says. My mother flinches at the Lord's name. "He is sooo cute! You didn't tell me he was so cute, David," she says. She holds her hand out and he sniffs.

Mother is rooting around in the kitchen. She finds a glass and fills it with orange juice. Goliath trots down the hallway.

"We'll be running along," Mother says, "just as soon as your father's out of the bathroom."

"Could be awhile," I say to Sandy.

"Not funny," Mother says. "We brought you up to respect your elders."

"Does Goliath have to go to the bathroom?" Sandy asks.

I can hear him breathing heavy in the bedroom, rooting through something. "He'll be okay," I say. "We'll take him for a walk later."

My father emerges from the bathroom. "Hey, Davey," he says. "Thanks so much for taking care of your old buddy there."

We exchange the usual pleasantries and they make to leave. Goliath runs in from the bedroom. He nuzzles my father's leg. Sandy rubs his head. "He is just adorable," she says.

"So are you over here…a lot?" Mother asks.

"We're dating, Mom," I say. "That's what people do when they date."

Mother packs her purse and my father stands by the door. While all this is going on, Goliath nudges my leg. He looks at Sandy and then back at me. He shakes his head. His mouth is set in a frown. The look in his eyes is something between anger and sadness.

"In sin?" he mouths.

Goliath punishes me by cuddling up to Sandy. We take him for a walk and he stays by her side. She throws a stick and he retrieves it, tail wagging.

When we make dinner he sits on her side of the table. She drops him scraps of tofu. He eats them, wags, begs for more.

"Maybe he's a vegetarian," she says, rubbing his head.

He smiles and gives me the look.

Later, we're watching *The Godfather* on DVD and Goliath curls up with Sandy, lays his big head in her lap. She rubs his ears and he wags his tail.

When Sonny is driving across the Jersey wasteland, I look over. Sandy is asleep. Goliath is watching me. "Living in sin," he says. He tries to whisper but he can't. "For shame, Daaaavey."

Sandy wakes up. "What the fuck," she says. I point to the television. Sonny is getting whacked at the tollbooth.

Goliath jumps off the couch and lies down on the carpet. "Look at that," Sandy says, "Goliath doesn't like the shooting. It's okay, baby." She rubs his head and he wags. Soon, he is face down on the carpet, his paws in front of his snout.

"Awwww...so cute," Sandy whispers. She thinks he's sleeping off the walk, but I know what he's doing. He's praying. And not for a sunny day or a T-bone or a longer walk tomorrow. He's praying for us. He's praying for our mortal souls.

"Did you give me a, uh, Creed CD?" Sandy says.

"Creed? What are you talking about?"

She throws a CD case on the counter. Creed. *Human Clay.* "This was in my car," she says.

"Shit," I say.

Sandy has had too much wine. She's wedged into a corner of the sofa, snoring lightly. She's wearing shorts and a tank top and I can't help but stare at her.

"We need to talk, Daaaavey," Goliath says.

This is what I was afraid of.

"It's David now," I say.

"You'll always be Daaaaavey to me, Daaaaavey," he says. It's been so long I forgot how irritating that voice was, the way he pulls his syllables out so slowly, over-pronounces everything, like a carnival barker on barbiturates.

"Things are different now. I'm different."

"I think you might be lost, Daaaavey," he says. His big face, square and earnest, looks up at me.

"I'm not lost. I'm happy. Finally. Look at that." I wave at Sandy, her adorable face smushed into the sofa. Even her drool is cute.

"It's like the time we were lost in that silver mine, Daaaavey," he says. "You remember, Daaaavey?"

"That was a long time ago."

"And I told you we didn't need a light. That God's light shone on us no matter where we were. Even in the deepest, darkest place, even when it seems like nobody cares."

Sandy rubs her eyes. "What's going on?" she says.

Goliath puts his head down and pretends to be sleeping.

I point to the TV. Jon Stewart makes a face and the studio audience roars.

Sandy rubs my leg. "Let's go to bed," she says.

It was around puberty when I started to drift away from Goliath, away from the church. Before, I wanted to be with him all the time. But a thirteen-year-old boy wants to be alone in the bathroom, in the mall, on the bus to middle school.

When the show was finally over, all I wanted to do was distance myself from *Davey and Goliath,* from the church, the family, the whole thing. It's not easy growing up a child star. You add the church thing in there: even worse. The family thing, it's almost impossible to live a normal life.

I see that Harry Potter kid in the tabloids today— chasing women, appearing naked in some play—and I understand completely.

I'm frying eggs when Sandy and Goliath get back from their walk. She hands him a treat, fills his water bowl. "Have you seen my birth control?" she says.

Goliath whines. I stare at him, trying to make eye contact.

"So have you seen it?" she says. "Weirdest thing, I can't find it anywhere."

"Must be up there somewhere," I say.

"Weird," she says.

Goliath walks into the living room and lies down.

"Fuck," I say.

She goes upstairs, comes back down a minute later. She throws a Bible on the counter. "What are you trying to do here?" she says. "You wanna start going to church again, just tell me. This is getting creepy, David."

"It's not me," I say. "You don't understand."

Goliath waddles up, rubs his head against her legs.

"Oh, really. Who is it then?" she says.

I don't know what to say.

She walks back upstairs. Goliath follows.

"Pray with me, Daaaavey," Goliath says.

Sandy is out shopping. Her sister, Allie, is coming for dinner.

"I'm not going to pray with you, Goliath," I say.

"You *are* lost, Daaaavey," he says.

"I am not. I'm home."

He lies down, puts his paws together over his nose. "Dear Jeeeeesus," he says, "Daaaavey is lost again. Please help Daaaavey, Jeeeesus. Help him find the light. Like that time we were lost in the old silver mine and I said…"

"You gotta stop this," I say. "I can't have this shit going on much longer."

"What are you talking about?" he says. His eyes are so innocent, so sure.

"The whole thing. The praying, the birth control, the fucking Creed CD."

"You think I'm just going to sit here and let you commit these siiiiiins," he says. "I can't let you do that to yourself, Daaaaavey. I love you. God loves you."

I stand there for a moment. Our eyes are locked. I think about all we've been through, the little "adventures," as my mother calls them. But those weren't real, I remind myself. They were scripted, written by the Lutheran church, for God's sake.

"It stops now," I say. Before he can respond, I go outside. I hose down the cooler and make sure we have enough gas in the grill. From the lawn, I can hear his mumbling, the rising and lowering of his voice, pleading for my soul.

"And you won't believe what this one stuck in my car as a joke," Sandy says. She finishes her beer and throws the Creed CD onto the picnic table. Allie howls. She is, like her sister, not a Creed kind of girl.

"So seriously," Allie says. "I was half-thinking there might be some kind of announcement or whatever, you know..."

"What?" Sandy says.

Goliath's ears prick up. He sits, wags his tail. After a whole evening of moping, he is finally coming to life.

"You know," Allie says. "Like some kind of...ring...or whatever."

"Oh god," Sandy says. She laughs, quick, like a snort, and punches me in the knee. "Not yet. Nothing yet, Al. Premature. Just the sin. The living in sin is going nicely."

Goliath lies down again. He tucks his head between his paws.

"Bathroom," Sandy says. She finishes her beer, and goes into the house.

Goliath follows.

"You want it, you got it," Allie says. She pushes the Creed CD into the player. Soon enough, we're singing along: "*Can you take me higher?*" we sing, each of us doing our drunk imitation of the singer's sober imitation of Eddie Vedder. "*To a place where blind men see? Can you take me higher? To a place with golden streets.*"

Something crashes and we turn off the music. Everything is quiet inside. "What was that?" I say, standing, already running into the house. Sandy is in a heap at the bottom of the stairs. Goliath sits next to her.

"Pray with me, Daaaavey," he says.

"I will not!" I say. There's something in his eyes. "You did this," I say.

"Who are you talking to?" Allie says.

Sandy is not moving. Goliath wags his tail once, looks me in the eye. I get down on my knees.

"What are you doing?" Allie says.

"I'm praying," I say.

WHERE WE'RE GOING

THERE ARE ONE, TWO, THREE, four...thirteen different kinds of lettuce. When the hell did this happen? I almost ask the lady next to me, then realize I look out of place enough with my paint-spattered boots, jeans, and T-shirt, with my fingers covered in drips and drops and my smell of turpentine and all-day sweat. So I stand there like a moron, a thirty-year-old man confused by vegetables. How am I supposed to make the decision—"where we're going" is how she puts it—when I can't even pick out lettuce at the goddamn supermarket?

I try to be cool, my eyes twitching back and forth between the lettuce and the little signs: "Green Leaf $1.49," "Butterhead $3.49," "Romaine," "Radicchio," "Arugula." It goes on and on, a wall of little green heads laughing at me. Some of these don't look like lettuce at all. They look like weeds. And there's spinach mixed in here. I always thought spinach was a whole other thing. Is it possible I was wrong all this time about spinach?

If I've been wrong about spinach, what the hell else have I been wrong about?

I've been painting baseboards all day and my knees ache, my back is tightening up. Jesus, I need to get out of this supermarket. This is fancier than I remember, with all this lettuce and the wide-open aisles, lights so bright I can feel a headache moving up my neck.

She's been gone eight days, and for the first time I wonder if I did the right thing, waiting like this, putting her off when I kind of knew the whole time, forcing her to do something because I was just too lazy or whatever to get it done.

Eight days and I haven't done a thing, haven't picked up a guitar, written a note, a word. Haven't even listened to anything other than the stupid Taylor Swift album, which was about the only thing she left behind.

A blonde with big hips and a little white skirt bustles down the aisle. Her bra straps peek out along her shoulders. I drift along behind, watching that skirt punch back and forth. When she picks up a bunch of bananas and half turns, I pretend to be staring real hard at the broccoli. I wonder if I should say something and what I would say. She wiggles toward the frozen food and I wander back to the lettuce.

For the first few days I was listening to the Taylor Swift out of meanness, making fun of it in my head, telling the walls about the cheesy synths and the bubble-gummy way the guitars sounded. About the picture on the cover and how long did it take to get her hair to fly around just perfect like that, the songs about boyfriends and breaking up and getting back together and you belong to me and forever and always and all of this from a girl who doesn't look old enough to drive.

The place is swirling all around me. I thought the grocery store would be deserted. Instead, housewives hustle by with screaming kids, young dudes stride around in suits, teenyboppers giggle in their hundred-dollar jeans. They all seem to know what kind of lettuce suits their needs.

Finally I grab a familiar-looking one that says "Iceberg" and head down the aisle. I make it a couple rows over, then realize that's exactly what she would say I'd probably do. That was one of her main points: that I don't want to try anything, have any "new experiences."

So I go back and grab the first new lettuce experience I see—one of those premade bags that says "Parisian Mix" in fancy letters. It's got some green leafy ones and some red ones that look like flower petals, plus some purple stuff that reminds me of confetti. That's a new goddam experience. I stomp toward the lunch meat, let my boots echo off the floor.

But then I feel the change in my pocket and remember I have about ten bucks until Friday. I turn around, feeling the heat crawl up my cheeks, walking a little lighter. I throw the Parisian Mix down and grab the iceberg. There's some lady there who sees me do it but I don't even look at her. The last thing I need now is that half-sorry smile, some kind of pity party for the guy who can't figure out the lettuce.

Tell the truth, iceberg's what she usually brought home, so I don't know what she's talking about when she says I'm not willing to experience new things. I was the one at home, waiting for the lettuce; the one out painting

71

houses, getting money for the lettuce. She was the one in here with all these new experiences, the one that kept bringing home iceberg. The one that kept listening to that one CD on a constant loop, some teenager never even bought her own lettuce in her entire life, singing about forever.

Something smells good in here and I realize I haven't eaten since the hot dogs at lunch. My stomach hurts and my hands are getting tingly.

I wonder what she's eating tonight. Probably her mom's still cooking for her, or else she's moved on already, put me behind her, looking to repay the hospitality with her big specialty: chicken and dumplings. My mouth starts to water and that pisses me off even more. It's like she's put some virus in me—fed it into my body real slow over time—and I can't get it out.

But should you marry somebody, be with her forever and always, if she's willing to leave you over something as stupid and made-up as getting married?

I look at my cart. Ten minutes and the iceberg is all I have to show for it. I know what I'm doing, poking around like this, but what the hell am I gonna do, anyway, when I get home?

Sometime after the first few days, the Taylor Swift started my toes tapping and I knew most of the words and I realized it was pretty good background music for me being angry and dicked over just like Taylor Swift was sometimes.

I'm even starting to miss the smell of her smoke. Kool Lights. Menthol. There are worse smells.

I don't know where the lunch meat is, so I wander along, watching the moms and the kids, wondering when the moms got so young and the kids got so loud. I turn down the cereal aisle and stop in my tracks. I never saw so many cereals in my life. If you asked me to do nothing but write down cereal ideas for a full year, I couldn't come up with some of this stuff. Blueberry Crunch Granola Flakes. Morning Cluster Poppers. Soy Crispy Pokey Flakes. What happened to Wheaties? What happened to Cookie Crisp?

I'm starting to think this isn't where she's been buying food all this time. I don't recognize any of this stuff. But I see people walking out with those plastic bags, blue see-through with a big "S" on the side. We have a whole closet full of those bags. She won't let me throw them away, says we have to recycle. Every now and then I toss a handful into the trash before I move it out to the curb. I do it fast, my hands flying like I'm masturbating.

All I really want is some Cocoa Puffs, but I feel like I should apologize to somebody for it. There's a woman in front of me—pretty, young, dressed up in a business suit with nice legs and her hair pulled tight into a bun. She's wearing those dork glasses, but on her they look sexy, like a secretary in a porn movie. She's looking at wheat, oats, and cranberry somethingorother. She takes four boxes of the stuff. It's on sale for $4.99. Twenty bucks on cereal.

I decide to skip breakfast. It's never been a big meal for me anyway. I'd only been eating it because she thought it was pitiful how little attention I paid to my body.

It was maybe the most pitiful thing about me, once you got her going on specifics. "It is pitiful the shit you put into your body," she'd say. "Your body is your temple."

"My temple likes Cocoa Puffs," I'd say, reading the back of the box instead of the newspaper, because I knew that pissed her off, too.

"There's an asshole living in your temple."

I never did come up with a decent comeback for that one.

That's fifteen minutes and all I have is this head of lettuce. I need some ham but the deli counter is crowded and I stand there a full ten minutes, waiting to get waited on, until I realize there's a number system and everybody has one but me.

There's a nice lady in front of me, looks about fifty, chubby, with hair dyed too black. She offers to let me go ahead, says she knows I was there before her and isn't it hard sometimes to figure if you're supposed to take a number.

I smile and say thanks but no thanks. Then I take a number and wait for a couple of minutes. People are ordering four or five meats at a time. They're getting cheeses and salads and chicken wings. They're buying by the pound, for today and tomorrow and goddamn forever and always, from the looks of it.

I don't think I want to be married, but I don't think I want to be here either. I wonder what she's doing right now. I crumple the number and stick it in my back pocket.

For the past couple days, I've been listening to the Taylor Swift on purpose, just like she did. I've been sitting in her chair, eating her Special K because my body is a temple. I've been looking at my guitar case in the corner, dusty because she refused to clean it, cleaned around it, even, the one time a month when she did clean. I know what the chords are on "Fifteen" and that one about the horses. I know I could play them if I wanted. I know how they'd sound, the progression, how my voice would kind of hum along with the words and then I'd sing the choruses and try to sing them scratchy and soft like Willie Nelson but it would just sound like me anyway.

I walk toward the checkout. The iceberg rolls around in the cart. I feel like everybody is staring at me, a big guy with a big cart and one head of lettuce. Ten bucks in my pocket and an empty house with *Fearless* on repeat. I get in line behind an old lady with a long gray ponytail.

She took most of the liquor, too, left a few beers that are long gone. You want to drink enough to fall asleep early, ten bucks won't last long. You want to sit around the house and pick at the paint spots on your fingernails, wonder what the hell you got yourself into, what you got yourself out of, listen to her music until you like it so much you think you're going crazy, you can stretch it out a good long time.

The old lady is next in line and she puts one of those plastic dividers after her stuff. I put my lettuce behind it because it seems like she's waiting for me to do it.

"You can go over there if you want to, dear," she says, pointing to the express line.

"That's okay," I say. I pick up a magazine with a picture of a skinny girl in a bikini on the cover. I page around, skim over an article about two movie stars who say they're in love, pictures of some actress dancing on tables, reviews of albums by groups I never heard of before. There's an article about Taylor Swift and some bad-boy racecar driver, but I don't have to read it to know it isn't true. I know those songs and I know she wouldn't get near that kid with a ten-foot pole. I know Taylor Swift will be just fine. Just then, the chorus to "Fifteen" comes up in my head and I get a tear in my eye and I have to stop and think about tomorrow's job—a new house in some new development, thirty-five hundred square feet and they want it all in Duron Mushroom White—just so I can get my legs back under me.

I wonder how late this grocery store stays open—if I could read all these magazines, catch up on what I've been missing all this time painting houses and going home to piss her off by not wanting to experience any new things or get married either.

The truth is the Taylor Swift is in the truck now and I'm looking forward to listening again.

All around me, people are loading their groceries. They are buying all kinds of stuff, two three four five at a time. They are thinking ahead, loading in provisions. I stand and wait and listen to the blips and the hum. She's probably at her mom's house still. She's probably on a date. In a few years, she'll be one of these women, buying the five-dollar cereal and the salad in the bag. My lettuce rolls around on the conveyor belt. A dozen people are lined up behind me. In front, the old lady's groceries are getting scanned and bagged, scanned and bagged. The conveyor belt keeps moving along and I poke at my lettuce when it lags behind. I keep my head down and wait.

FREE WILL

WE WERE MULLETED and we aspired to beards. Thick beards that trailed down our necks like former East Shickelimmy Fighting Miners power forward Kevin Yustat, or stubble like former point guard Ron Bongo, or even the straggly, mustache-heavy half-beard sported by former center Jerry Caviston. Toss in the goatees of twin guards Bill and Bob Bomboy, and the entire Miners starting five had been rather spectacularly bearded. We, the new starting five, were as bare as the court on which we'd suffer our most public failures.

Our coach was a ruddy-faced descendant of coalminers who talked about "mental toughness" the way old hippies referred to Woodstock. On the night we became the starting five, he was bellied up to the bar at Stoney's, deep into a fourth pitcher with Old Snyder, the girl's tennis coach. It was Young Snyder, a cop no more than four years out of Shickelimmy High himself, who busted the party. He was new and looking to make a name and he only thought to call Coach after he had the starting five locked up in the Barney Fife little cell in the jail next to the hardware store. We had been in the middle of our best season ever—15 and 2, with a firm grip on the Anthracite League championship—and Young Snyder may have been stupid and brash and blinded by ambition, but even he eventually figured out that he had a situation on his hands.

We were not called. Not summoned. We were not needed. We were poised on the edge of manhood and we were smart enough to tilt in the other direction, toward the green fields of boyhood and Kool-Aid, of Wiffle ball and Ultraman, Dungeons and Dragons and the hard rock philosophy of Canadian power trios.

And so at twelve thirty on Saturday night, we were neither bellied up at Stoney's nor drunk and blasting AC/DC in the middle of some farmer's field (too close to Route 32, as it turned out). We were holed up in Reese's basement with a treasure chest of Mr. Pibb and Funyons, Rush blaring on the stereo, engaged in an epic game of Dungeons and Dragons. We were deep in the game. We were not us. We were knights. Henchmen. Wanderers and Sorcerers. We were named Murlynd, Robilar, Tenser, Tarik, Yrag, Bigby, Melf. We were ancient and adult, ruddy and muscled and bearded like Vikings. We were listening to "Tom Sawyer," the first song on Rush's new album, on a permanent loop.

And so, at the very moment when we became the starting five, we were not even of this world. Time had gone fuzzy. Until Mr. Reese came home from Stoney's and burst into the basement on a riptide of Marlboro Reds and Yuengling.

"You guys aren't gonna believe it!" he said. "Holy shit. Sorry. No, holy shit. You all little sonsabitches are

the starting team now. The whole fucking lot of 'em—
Bomboys, Yustat, Caviston, Bongo, shit, even Cordas and
Reitz—they're all in jail."

We stood, chugged our Mr. Pibb in nervous gulps, our
heads coming up through the fog of centuries, honing in
on this strange and terrifying news.

"You guys are gonna be the fucking starting team!"
Mr. Reese said. He moved into the room and awkwardly
hugged Rodney, his son. "Let me introduce you to the
new starting power forward of the Shickelimmy Fighting
Miners!" he said, and then he tried to make Rodney shake
his hand, as if he were conferring a knighthood.

"You're drunk, Dad," Rodney said.

"And you boys better get ready," he said. He looked at
the battle lined up on the card table, our polyhedral dice
and charms, Funyons and Mr. Pibb. "Clean up this shit
and get some sleep. You're gonna need it." He let out a
drunken whoop and clambered upstairs.

We stared at each other, at the little pieces on the card
table, which suddenly looked like nothing but what they
were—children's toys, something that belonged to a time
we had only just stumbled out of, gawky and premature.

"What the heck?" said Bailey. He was the new center—
six foot three and one hundred twenty-five pounds. He
seemed to be shrinking into himself, hunching even more
than usual. "That can't be right. Your dad's drunk, right?"
He looked at Reese, who was sitting on the floor, trying
to get used to the fact that although he had never played
more than three minutes in a single game, and every one
of them had come after the Fighting Miners were already

thirty points ahead or behind, he was now the starting power forward.

"Who do we play on Tuesday?" Benner asked. He was the new point guard, a pesky little defender who never lost his dribble and never, ever took a shot, and the only one of us who had ever seen real minutes in an actual game. He had a look in his eye like he had just won a pet lion—happy, proud, and scared to death.

"Tuesday?" Kenner said. "We have to play on freakin' Tuesday?"

"Milton," Hoak said.

We sat in our chairs or the floor, fingering our charms. We picked our cuticles and wished we were tired, wished we hadn't all told our parents we were sleeping over at Reese's house, wished we could slink up to our rooms, pull the covers over our heads, and bawl like the little boys we were.

What we did was go over the offense. Benner was the first to come out of his funk. Reese got a basketball from the garage. We never let that ball touch the floor. Something was flowing through us then—fear, mainly fear, but also something else, a sense that we had crossed some kind of line and whether we were remotely ready or not, from here on out things were going to be different.

"You're gonna have to be mentally tough," Coach said.

He was pacing, screaming, delirious at the prospect of watching his 15 and 2 season slip away to a bunch of untested boys with mullets and pimples and not a razor among us. We were lined up along the baseline, the five of us who had previously made up the junior varsity feeling dreamy and uncomfortable in our varsity blue practice jerseys, the ninth-grade team beaming and nervous in their junior varsity reds.

"I'm not…I'm not…" Coach said, and then he paused, looked at the basket, jumped up and touched the net, and continued, "I'm not giving this season up." We nodded, tried to look convincing. If only we could get out of this scene, if we could play the role of Hardened Basketball Team Receiving Pep Talk, maybe this would all go away. Maybe it was a dream, or maybe it would work, or maybe it wouldn't be as bad as we thought.

"Todd Benner, I can see you believe!" Coach said.

"We're ready, Coach!" Benner said. Point guard until the end.

"This is going to be okay," Coach said. "We're going to get those sonsabitches at Milton, aren't we?"

We bellowed, screamed. Never had we yelled so loudly. Inside, we hoped that if we pleased him in this way he would call practice early, let us go home to our beds and our *Lord of the Rings* books. We would ball into celebration, high five, wipe the imaginary sweat from our brow, take a well-earned shower, and go on home. But Coach had different ideas.

"First team," he said. "Half court. Second team!" He nodded at the ninth-graders. "Defense!"

We were terrible. Distracted and nervous. Even the sure-handed Benner dribbled the ball off his feet, threw inbounds passes into empty bleachers. We were decimated by the ninth-graders, fourteen to two in ten minutes of live scrimmage. One ninth-grader in particular, Ricky Nicholls, scored twelve points on his own. He sunk thirty-footers and driving layups, twisting ten-footers and offensive put-backs. Once he seemed dangerously close to dunking. He drove the lane and dished to less-than-sure-handed ninth-graders who let his passes bounce of their hands, necks, and faces. Coach whistled and stood silent, watching Ricky Nicholls take us apart like he was the unholy offspring of Dr. J and Rick Barry.

By the end of the scrimmage, Nicholls was on our side, having replaced Kenner, and was bouncing passes off our hands, necks, and faces. We looked at each other and we didn't need to talk.

"Okay," Coach said, calling us all in. He gave Ricky Nicholls a nod. "I think we might be all right."

"I don't like him," Hoak said. "He seems stuck up."

"Where did he come from?" Kenner said.

We were listening to Rush again. Geddy Lee singing about free will. The tape clicked and Reese hit rewind.

"Geez, Reese," Hoak said. "Let's at least listen to a different song."

"Where did he come from?" Reese said.

"I never saw him before," Benner said. He was the only of us who felt confident enough in his skills to play basketball with other people outside the season. "I heard he moved last year and broke his ankle during buck season. Then he didn't heal up until now, I guess."

"You guys wanna play D&D?" Reese said.

We did want to play D&D. We really did. Each and every one of us, save perhaps Benner. In the Old Greywolf

Castle, we were not skinny and underweight power
forwards, guards who could never remember to rotate
down to cover the baseline when the ball swung to the
corners, centers who couldn't make so much as a simple
layup with our left hand. We never dribbled the ball off
our feet or let our defenders muscle us into the corners
or forgot to set the pick in the motion offense. We were
knights, elves, kings. We were dangerous and magical.
There was nothing we would have liked better than a
junk-food buffet and a dungeon battle to the theoretical
death. We looked at him like he was crazy.

Tuesday came fast. Milton was last year's Anthracite
League champions. They were tall and lanky, with a
six-two point guard, a six-six center, and everything in
between. They were four seniors and a junior, not the
most talented players, but they were grinders, the kind of
kids who waited around, lifted weights, got slowly bigger
and stronger until that one thing—bigger and stronger—
was good enough. They had stubble and hairy legs and a
medieval giant's plodding and impossible force, and they
beat us eighty-four to thirty-two. Ricky Nicholls scored
twenty-four points, with twelve rebounds and four assists.
For the rest of us, dungeon masters and elves and knights
and princes, the math was all too easy: we had scored a
total of eight points.

"Jeepers, cats!" Coach said afterward, pacing the
locker room floor. We sat on creaky benches, heads down.
"Mental toughness! Ricky can't…. It's…mental toughness!

Mental..." He trailed off, lit a cigarette, sat down in a folding chair.

We tried not to cry, watching him smoke that entire cigarette and then light another. We sat there until we were sticky and cold and then followed him out to the bus. We rode the entire hour home in clammy silence. No one, not even Benner, said a single word.

Ricky Nicholls was not like us. He was driven, focused, single-minded. We had never seen him before because he was not to be found at the mall or the movies, the comic-book shop or the Tastee Freeze or the roller rink or any of the other places we pursued our boyish interests. He was rumored to spend nearly every waking hour playing pick-up basketball at the local college, stroking his sweet jump shot, pulling rebounds away from frat boys, driving the line and bouncing passes off the hands, necks, and faces of guys who were, some of them, old enough to drink, who (we guessed) regularly had sex, who had presumably left their dungeons and their dragons back home in Parsippany or Bethesda or Deer Park, Long Island.

He lifted weights, ran even when he didn't have to, and was rumored to be on some kind of macrobiotic diet.

"That's bullshit. I've seen him eat pizza," Benner said. Benner, point guard to the end, was inclined to stick up for Ricky Nicholls, who by now was fully cemented in place as our best player and worst enemy. Not only was he starting at the two guard, leading the team in points, steals, rebounds, and floor burns, but he had also been designated as "mentally tough" by Coach, an unofficial title that carried with it the official title of Team Captain. The Shikelimmy Daily Press had done a feature story with the headline "Fresh-Man Among Boys."

The message was clear across the board. Ricky Nicholls was a basketball-playing man. The rest of us were rosy-cheeked, balls-bouncing-off-our-heads-necks-and-faces boys. That it was true didn't help at all in our coming to grips with this situation.

Ricky Nicholls didn't help, either. He ignored us in the hallways, begrudgingly accommodated our occasional requests for high or low fives, jabbing his talented digits for a quick slap and then retracting immediately, as if he didn't trust us with this basic gesture any more than he trusted us to corral his no-look passes before they caromed off our hands, necks, and faces.

"I'm telling you," Hoak said, "he's stuck up. Coach thinks he's the man and he believes it."

We were sitting around a picnic table at the Tastee Freez. It was Saturday night and we hadn't played D & D since Reese's father had burst into the game and changed our world.

"He's like a Stormtrooper," Reese said.

"More like an orc," said Bailey.

"Kind of just like an orc," Hoak said.

We sat pondering the orc-ness of our phenom teammate.

"So what are we gonna do?" Benner said. "I mean, this stinks. We have to do something. Get better. Practice more."

Reese turned up his boom box. He had taken to playing the cassette tape with "Free Will" by Rush on an endless loop. "We have options," he said.

"What are you talking about?" Hoak said.

Reese just pointed at the box. Geddy Lee's elfin and commanding voice exploded: "You can choose a ready guide in some celestial voice," he sang.

"God, Reese," Hoak said. "Give it a rest."

The starting five got out of jail but they never came back to school. We heard they had gotten jobs, that they were on probation, that Bongo's college scholarship offers had been rescinded and that Yustat had nearly killed a full-grown man in the county lockup. We didn't know if any of it was true—until Yustat showed up at practice.

Coach met him with a hug and we stopped in our tracks. Yustat looked older. He had grown out his beard and appeared to have gained weight. He was wearing a flannel shirt and jeans stained with cement dust or mulch or something from one of the other hourly wage jobs that were regularly held out by our parents as the kind of worst-case scenario awaiting the perpetrator of unfinished geometry homework.

"Boys!" Coach called. "Everybody gather round." His voice was soft and sad, a tone we had never heard from him before. It was as if Geddy Lee opened his mouth and sounded like Barry White. It made no sense at all.

Yustat tapped a dusty boot and fingered his keys. He nodded to Ricky Nicholls and examined the rest of us.

"I'm real proud of you guys," he said. "Real proud." We flashed on snapped towels, purple nurples, wet willies, the indelible inside-the-locker view of a door slamming shut. "I mean it," he said. "I know we had some fun with you guys, gave you a little hazing. Shit, we all went through that." He smiled, his eyes scanned the row of district championship banners that hung along the top wall. He shook his head, looked at his boots on the gym floor.

"Kevin," Coach said.

"Sorry," he said. "The point is, I'm proud of you. We're all proud of you. You ain't winning much but you're young and trust me—this shit you're going through, getting your butts kicked around, it'll wind up being the best thing for you. In the long run."

He trailed off and Coach patted him on the back. "Thanks, Kevin," he said. "That means a lot. To the guys."

They walked over to the stairs together, Coach's arm around Yustat's shoulder. We stole glances at each other and then quickly looked away. "Let's go," Benner said, and we all followed him down to the baseline and started our laps.

The games rolled on and the losing continued. We were exhausted, beaten, our bodies covered in black and blue, our ankles and knees and elbows in tape. We lost weight or gained it. For the very first time in our lives, we went to bed early and had trouble getting to sleep. We drank coffee and soda and wondered what relief the starting five had found out in those cornfields with their Busch and dime bags. We counted the games and watched our record tip steadily toward five hundred.

Shamokin would be the last game of the season. Our record was fifteen and twelve, and we were on the brink of elimination from the playoffs. "A win and we're in," Coach said on the bus to Shamokin. "One win and it's playoffs and anything can happen." He had taken to thinking positive, to shouting "I'm gonna make men out of you yet!" and slapping our butts with grim enthusiasm, to singing along when Reese blared "Free Will" through the locker room. Something in him seemed to have gone wacky, like his body had been replaced by a positive-thinking pod that had been programmed to get one win and then get in.

Shamokin's gym was large and terrifying, lit bright yellow, and reverberating with AC/DC's "Highway to Hell" and the grumbles of laid-off coalminers who peopled the stands in various strains of flannel and denim. By this point the games didn't frighten us the way they had in the beginning. We had become immune to the twice-weekly beatings administered throughout Central Pennsylvania's class AA high schools. We evolved from numb surprise to numb resolve, and we approached this final game with a forward-thinking determination usually reserved for root-canal patients.

On this night our warm-ups were robotic, dreamlike. Even Ricky Nicholls seemed shaken and nervous. The Shamokin fans were rabid and angry, chanting and singing along with Bon Scott and the Young boys.

In the locker room before tipoff, Reese blared "Free Will" and Coach just sat there, staring at us, moving down the line, boy to boy to boy in a stare-off that we knew was intended to evoke our inner mental toughness. "That song," he said. "Think about it. 'You can choose a ready guide in some celestial voice. If you choose not to decide you still have made a choice. You can choose from'…whatever, I don't quite get that next part. But here's the thing: 'I will choose a path that's clear. I will choose free will!'"

We sat there, stunned. He was listening to that all along? Paying attention to the lyrics? To Rush?

"You can choose," he said quietly. "You. Can. Choose." He walked down the row, poked each one of us in the chest. "You." Poke. "Can." Poke. "Choose." Poke. Then he turned and walked into the gym. We didn't know what else to do, so we followed.

The first half was the best sixteen minutes of our nascent basketball lives. We nailed jumpers, connected on wild half-court passes, managed to catch Ricky Nicholls' missiles before they slapped into our hands, necks, and faces. Shamokin stayed with us. They were bigger, stronger, mentally tougher. They were a plodding, half-court team, moving the ball around the perimeter, searching for angles, exposing a crack here, a missed assignment there, banking fifteen-footers or lining perfect bounce passes to waiting big men, who knocked in layups with lumbering efficiency. In response, we ran, got out on the break and converted three-on-twos, two-on-ones. Benner pulled up at the foul line and nailed his first jump shot of the year. Ricky Nicholls gave them fits on the perimeter, first hitting jumpers from the corners, then pump faking and taking it to the hoop.

At halftime we were tied thirty to thirty and the Shamokin faithful were roiling like fish in a bucket. They might as well have been calling for the sacrifice of a virgin. Or of five virgins.

Coach bounded into the locker room. He pointed to Reese. Power chords. Drums. Geddy Lee's strangely inspirational voice filled the room. Coach nodded and tapped his feet. We were confused, scared. Was this what we were capable of, had been all along? Could this possibly continue? Everything we knew about ourselves was in flux, changing, changed. Was this free will?

Right away we knew they were angry. They came out swinging, elbows and asses poking and jabbing at our soft places. They dove at passes, scurried into the stands, accrued court burns like Pac-Men eating dots. We played in a daze, still running and gunning, knocking down ill-advised twenty-footers and double clutch reverse layups, tossing blind over-the-shoulder passes to surprised teammates streaking down the lane. Through it all, that song echoed in our heads: *I will choose a path that's clear. I will choose free will.*

With one minute left in the fourth quarter, we were down forty-nine to forty-eight and Coach called timeout. We walked to the bench and sat in a daze, sweat dripping off our dewy faces. "Okay, guys," Coach said. And then he stopped. He stared at the stands and our eyes followed.

There they were. The starting five. Yustat. Caviston. Bongo. The Bomboys. There was Cordas and Reitz. All of the seniors. They were clad in their letterman's jackets, standing, applauding. There was something in their faces— they were not smiling, not happy. They were proud. Coach nodded to Yustat, who had a rip in his sleeve, a red knot on his forehead, and blood dripping down into his beard. Yustat nodded back, gave the thumbs up. Coach smiled and then retreated back into our huddle.

"I told you I was gonna make men out of you," he said. "Now let's go finish this."

We jogged back to the court, the crowd's roar a thick rumble that set our dewy neck hairs on end. *You can choose a ready guide in some celestial voice.*

Benner passed to Ricky Nicholls. He dribbled, letting the clock run. Shamokin's point guard, a scrapper in tight shorts and a full mustache, forced him left. Ten seconds. Ricky dribbled behind his back and lost the point guard. He brought it to the foul line, juked, and headed for the lane. He went up and took Shamokin's center and power forward with him, and then slung a perfect behind-the-back pass to Reese.

Reese waited a beat. Pump faked. Pumped again. Then went up. He was fouled. Two shots. One second left. The din was incredible. It was like a plane warming up. The starting five remained standing, their arms crossed over their letterman's jackets. Their bearded faces tightened into grim expressions and you could see it, what they were going to look like in ten, fifteen, twenty years. There's Kevin Yustat on a barstool, puffy and angry, still haunted by those championship banners strung up in the high school gym. There's Jerry Caviston, punching in at the plant, talking Penn State football and Shikelimmy basketball on his lunch break. There's Ron Bongo in a Montgomery Ward suit, trading his high school quarterback status for a job hustling used cars. There are the Bomboys, working construction and living together, still woman-less, in some grim apartment. There they all are, grunting and sweating, bouncing beer belly to beer belly in some dusty rec league gym, digging elbows into rib cages, lunging after loose balls, struggling with everything in their failing bodies to evoke some thin ghost of their high school days.

If you choose not to decide you still have made a choice.

Reese walked to the line. He looked to the stands and then to each of us. He dribbled the ball twice and then paused, backed off the line. He drew a deep breath, dribbled twice again. He pulled back and heaved the basketball off the left side of the backboard.

Coach stood and walked to the scorer's table. He seemed to be considering something but he sat back down. Reese walked calmly to the line. He took the ball. He brought it between his legs and threw it as high into the air as he could. There was a gasp and then whistles blew, horns sounded, the crowd erupted. Zero seconds left. The Milton players looked at us with surprise, and then pity, and then they bunched into a circle and laughed and cried and shouted. In the stands, Yustat was still standing, alone. His eyes were closed and his head tilted back to the yellow lights. The blood from his nose trailed down into his beard. His arms dangled at his sides. He looked defeated, broken. We stole glances and walked off the court with our heads down, feeling naked and light and free.

INTERLUDE:
NOVELTY SONG

PAUL STANLEY SUMMARIZES THE TRAGEDIES OF WILLIAM SHAKESPEARE DURING BETWEEN-SONG BANTER FROM THE 1977-78 KISS ALIVE II TOUR

Assembly Center
Tulsa, Oklahoma
January 26, 1977

PAUL: Yeah! You all are crazy, Tulsa! I think...I think...I think Tulsa might be the craziest place we played ON THIS TOUR. That's right, Tulsa! You know what gets me crazy, Tulsa? You wanna *knooooooooow* what gets me *CRAAAAA-AAAAA-AAAA-ZEEEEEE*? I get craaaaazeeee when I see them young girls, Tulsa. I see 'em walkin' down the street so young and clean and I just can't help myself, people! Remind me of another young boy couldn't help himself when he saw them young girls. And I ain't talkin' about just anybody, Tulsa! I ain't talking about you...or me...or Peter or Ace or even Gene, people! I'm talking 'bout a man named Romeo, Tulsa! *ROOOOO-MEEEEEEE-OOOOOOH!* My man Romeo, he loved them young girls, Tulsa, oh YEAH, he loved 'em! And this one girl he loved her special. You know who I'm talkin' about...shout it out, Tulsa...tell me Romeo and...

AUDIENCE: JULIET!

PAUL: What you say, Tulsa? I can't HEEAAAR YOU.

AUDIENCE: JULIET!

PAUL: That's right, Tulsa. This song is about a Juliet all my own, a little girl named...CHRISTINE SIXTEEN!

Kemper Arena
Kansas City, Missouri
November 27, 1977

Thank you, Kansas City! Thank you! Ace Frehley on guitar, Kansas City! Yeah! Give it up, people! The Space Ace! Hold on now, Kansas City...let's bring it down now...let's bring it *doooooooown noooooow.* Let's bring it down 'cause I gotta talk about something now, Kaaaay Ceeeee...I gotta talk about love. Have you ever been in LOOOOOOOOOOOOOOVE? I said have you ever been in LOOOOOOOOOOOOOOOOOOOVE?!?! You ever been in that "can't get enough of each other, can't wait to see her, she can't wait to see me, I wanna sink ships, go to war, kill myself" love, Kansas City? I'm sayin' you ever been in *Antony-and-Cleopatra* love, people? Have you, Kansas City!?! When you in love like that, people, you know, only one thing in your mind, and it ain't walkin', it ain't talkin', it ain't your job or your mamma or your daddy, people! Only thing on your mind when you're in *Antony-and-Cleopatra* love, Kansas City, the only thing you're thinking is I WAS MADE...FOR LOVIN'...YOU!

Veterans Memorial Arena
Des Moines, Iowa
November 29, 1977

That's right, people! You wanted the best and you got it! We are the KINGS, Des Moines! The KINGS OF ROCK AND ROLL! Salute, Des Moines! Pray at the ALTAR, Des Moines! But I gotta talk to you about something tonight, Des Moines, because bein' the king ain't so easy, people. It ain't *eeeezeeeeeee*! You don't believe that, if you don't belieeeeeeve that, Des Moines, well then you can just check out my man Macbeth. I'm talkin' about pressure, Des Moines. I'm talking about *muuuuuuuurdeeeeeer and maaaaaaaadneeeeeessssssss*. I said *MURDER!* And I said *MAAADNESSSSSSS!* It ain't everybody can stand bein' the king is what I'm tellin' you people. But I'm here to tell you, Des Moines, that I'm the man ready for the job, Des Moines. I ain't no Macbeth, people. Because I...AM KING...OF THE NIGHTTIME WORLD!

Omaha Auditorium
Omaha, Nebraska
November 30, 1977

Yeah! Hotter than Hell! How you like that, Omahaaaaaaaaa! It's a hot night tonight! HOT! HOT! It is HOT here in the Omaha Auditorium and we gonna make it even HOTTER, ain't we, Omaha? AIN'T WE, OMAHA?!?! Let me tell you, Omaha, we're lucky to be hot tonight. Yeah! We're luuuuuuckeeeeeee. Some people out there, people, they ain't got nothing at all, living in the street, serving water for a meal. Warm water, Omaha! That ain't no feast! But that was a feast, people, that was a FEAST PEOPLE for my man Timon of Athens. That's right, Omaha! And everybody know, Omaha, that when you're out on the street for a living, they got you under their thumb, people! They got you under their THUMB, people! Can you give me the chorus? I said CAN YOU GIVE ME THE CHORUS? Whooo, Black Diamond!

St. Paul Civic Arena
St. Paul, Minnesota
December 2, 1977

St. Paaaaaaaauuuuuuuuuul! How we doing, St. Paul! You know KISS is always workin' overtime for you, people! We workin' like James Brown. Like O.J. Simpson, people! That's right, St. Paul! KISS is fighting a rock-and-roll war, brothers. We gonna build us a rock-and-roll city. We gonna take a lesson from a guy you mighta heard about, ST. PAAAAUUUUUL. A guy named Caesar! We gonna take a lesson and we gonna fight that war and we gonna watch our back and we gonna build that city. You know what that city is called, people? DO YOU KNOW WHAT THAT CITY IS CALLED?! It ain't Rome! It ain't

New York City. It ain't even St, Paul, people! That city is called...DETROIT! ROCK! CITY!

Dane County Expo Center Coliseum
Madison, Wisconsin
December 3, 1977

That was Gene Simmons, Madison! GENE SIMMONS! I gotta tell you, Madison. We been all over this country and there ain't nothin' like those good Madison, Wisconsin, women! Yeah! You know what I'm talking about, people! You know I seen women all over this world, people, and there ain't nothin' like a Midwest woman. Woooooo! One thing about a Madison woman, people, she always tells you what's on her mind. ON HER MIIIIIIIIND. Let me tell you about a straight shooter named Cordelia, people! She told it like it was. I'm talkin' 'bout no bullshit, people. She looked her daddy right in the eye and she told him how it was, people. And her daddy wasn't just any daddy, Madison. Her daddy was KING LEAAAAAR, Madison. Now I'm tellin' you what, people: you need a good woman like Cordelia around, Madison. A good WISCONSIN WOMAN because I'm tellin' you people...when that time comes...I'm sayin' when that times comes, people, and you gotta look your woman in the eye...you gotta look your woman in the eye, now, Madison, and you gotta ask her that question...that one question we all wanna know. I say I know you love my...LIMOUSINE! I say I know you love my...CREDIT CARDS! I know you love...ROCK AND ROLL! But I just got this one question, left, baby...one question for you, Madison...DO...YOU...LOVE...ME?!?

ROCK OUT, MATE

What Would Elvis Do?

I'm the fat one, the normal-looking one, the one who gives the girls some hope that if they ever got backstage or if DaWestSidaz actually went to their high school, they might have a chance. In the Academy's Formula, what I am is known as "Grounding." That's Looks, Sex, Danger, Sweetness, Grounding. DaWestSidaz breaks down like this: Looks = Ricky, Sex = DaJuan, Danger = Lionel, Sweetness = Johnny B, Grounding = Fabio.

People assume I'm the stupid one, too, because I hardly ever talk, stay in the background while Ricky sounds off about love or working out or how lucky we all feel to have been selected by Colonel Randy and how blessed we are to even be a part of DaWestSidaz. But I'm just as qualified as Ricky. All five of us have been at the Academy since we were twelve, had the same voice, dance, charisma, fashion, and media classes, spent the same holidays working on choreography or interview skills. But I'm the only one who knows how to play a guitar, the one who actually tries to write his own songs, who knows how lame it is to have a choreographer and three singing coaches and a team of guys we've never met who write every single note of every single song, who knows enough to be embarrassed that we'll be taking the stage, all five of us, with no instruments, recorded music blaring while we lip sync into our wireless microphones and dance like Miley Cyrus.

Unless you count Jasper the Roadie, I'm the only one in the whole operation who knows his rock-and-roll history well enough to realize how ironic it is that our manager calls himself tshe Colonel with no sense of irony whatsoever.

I'm also the only one who can see Jasper. The only one who can hear him now as he grumbles and jitters and smokes from his one-hitter as we slog through prep for yet another photo shoot. Colonel Randy is standing in the corner, watching the make-up girls' asses and bullying somebody on his cell. "That's not enough!" he shouts. He pounds the deli tray, shoves another piece of ham into his mouth, then hangs up. Jasper sits in the corner near the back, his Sex Pistols T-shirt ripped, his green hair falling out, as usual. He can't sit still and he hops and shakes his head like Joe Cocker in full rock possession spaz-out, every now and then smashing a hand silently against the wall and then recoiling in pain.

The make-up girl finishes with Lionel and sends him off to Hair. "Who's next?" she says, but it's not really a question, since I'm the only one left in the room.

"This one," Colonel Randy says, pointing at me. "And let's try to make him a little more presentable." Jasper makes a face and mimics the Colonel's affected mannerisms.

"I'm good," I say.

"You can be replaced, Flabbio," Colonel Randy says.

Jasper coughs a cloud of greenish smoke.

The room is all white, clean as a Jerry Garcia D chord. Like all the Academy buildings, the Make-up Wing is antiseptic and anonymous, like a high-end rehab center. Even when I was fresh out of Scranton, I knew something about this whole thing was wrong, too neat and ordered for real rock and roll.

"Ass in the chair," the Colonel says.

"You think John Lennon ever had to get blush applied?" I say. Jasper gives me the thumbs up. His thumb falls off and he picks it up, mumbles *bollocks*, and stuffs it back on.

"I knew John Lennon," the Colonel says.

"You *met* John Lennon," I say.

"You gonna make me go over the terms of your contract again?" he says. "You wanna tell Mama how she's gonna pay for that cripple brother without DWS money rolling in? Now is not the time, son."

I look at my Doc Martens while the red crawls up my neck. Jasper shakes his head in the corner.

"You know how easy it would be to find another fat kid who can sing?" the Colonel says. "I see fifty fat kids can sing a day. I get a hundred letters every day from fat kids can sing's parents. I let maybe one a year into the Academy, give them that privilege. And it is a privilege, son, even if me and your mama go way back, even though she's paying that tuition every year. This here is the Harvard of musical personality instruction, and you know it."

I take the eyeliner and apply it in big swoops along my eyes, Robert Smith style.

"And to be honest?" the Colonel says, "Some days I'm not so sure your mama's talent got passed on. Not so sure at all."

I grab the lipstick and dab a clown spot of blush on each cheek. Jasper giggles and pulls tabs of skin off his hands.

"That's how you want to look for this photo? Like one of those Good Charlotte clowns?"

I take the cuticle trimmer and rip a hole in my shirt.

"You know how many albums Lady Gaga sold last year?" Colonel Randy says. He gets that wheels-turning grin, the one I've come to hate. "I think you look perfect, son."

Elvis listened blindly to Colonel Tom Parker. He wound up a shell of himself, a paranoid neurotic living in the bloated husk of his body. He made his greatest music when he was twenty, spent his entire adult life systematically corrupting his own legend with paranoia, banana and bacon sandwiches, pills, girls, insulation, and bad advice.

I look to the back of the room. Jasper is gone. "Fucking wanker," I mumble, and make my way to Hair.

What Would Keith Richards Do?

Ricky is leading us in the post-rehearsal prayer when one of Colonel Randy's assistants steams into the studio. "We need all of you," she says. "Important."

"Come on, fellas," Ricky says. He pulls us tighter. I can smell his aftershave and strawberry gum. "And dear Lord," he says, eyes closed, bottom lip quivering, "help me and the boys have a kick-butt workout this afternoon."

We high five and proceed to the Wahlberg Meeting Room, where Johnny B's parents and sisters are waiting.

As soon as we get into the room, Johnny B breaks down. "I know, I know," he yells. He's sweating like James Brown, crying like a fifteen-year-old girl at the Beatles' Shea Stadium concert. He falls to the ground and his sisters surround him, cooing in soft Spanish. His father stands near the window, rubbing a hand along his chin and whispering with Colonel Randy.

Ricky joins the pile-on with Johnny B's sisters, who, of course, welcome him with open arms.

Lionel is crying, too. I can tell he wants to join in, probably wants to lower himself right onto Ricky, but he knows enough to stay in the background. DaJuan just shakes his head, wanders over to the windows, and watches the tween girls doing Diva Boot Camp out on Aguilara Field.

I look for Jasper in the corner, forget that this is the new wing and he can't come in here. He's relegated to the Timberlake Center, the part that used to be a recording studio and concert hall before Colonel Randy bought it and the adjoining land and created the Randy Academy for Musical Youth Development. The brochure still says, "The ghosts of Keith Richards and John Lennon linger in the original sections of the Academy."

Of course, Keith Richards isn't even dead yet, so it would be hard for his ghost to linger anywhere, and with Jasper bouncing around, we're kind of full up on rock-and-roll ghosts right now.

"Him?" I say to Lionel. "What is he addicted to?" But he's just watching Ricky, the desire plain on his face. I wonder if I haven't been giving Johnny B enough credit. Maybe he really is a rocker. I tick off the list of real artists who have been in the same situation: Hank, Keith, Janis, Jerry, Cash, Jennings, Gram, Crosby, Jimi, Lou, Sid, Kurt, Van Halen, Earle, Tweedy. I wonder how he even managed to get addicted to whatever—pot, meth, blow, Oxycontin, Adderall, heroin—with the Academy locked down from eight at night until eight in the morning, and even during the day manned security at every gate.

"Addicted to the Internet," Lionel whispers. "He's been checking Twitter like four hundred times a day."

"The Internet?" I say it too loud, and Colonel Randy shoots me a look.

Johnny B's father exhales, no doubt seeing visions of tuition fees in his head.

Born too late, I think.

The pile-on has reverted to some kind of group hug and they all keen around the conference room. All but Johnny B's little sister, Sandy, the one with the Tina Turner legs and the voice of Aretha. She is leaning against the window, popping her gum and writing in a moleskin journal. She hums something to herself, a soft melisma up and down the scale. I recognize the tune. It's "Skool Daze (Are Gonna Make Me Go Back 2 Lovin' U)," the only DWS song that I sing lead on. It's our rockiest tune, kind of *Thriller* meets *Exile on Main St.* Or at least that's how I like to think of it. It's bollocks is what Jasper says, but Jasper says that about almost everything.

Colonel Randy is shaking hands with Johnny B's father, nodding his head. They're both looking at Sandy and talking low.

Finally Randy coughs and steps forward. His face is the color of cotton candy and huge beads of sweat trickle down his jowls. He's clutching his Panama hat to his chest like a defibrillator.

"This is a terrible day," he says. "Addiction of any kind is the scourge of our modern society." He looks to the parents and I know he's thinking about the checks they've written every semester, year after year. "And what's happened to Johnny B is something I wouldn't wish on anybody. Johnny's going to have to go get the help he needs. Johnny's going to have to leave DaWestSidaz, people."

Keith Richards had a full-body transfusion to kick his heroin habit. David Crosby went to jail. Steve Earle, jail as well. Kurt Cobain blew his head off. Gram Parsons wound up in a pyre in the desert, even his funeral illegal and cool and legendary. Morrison and Moon and Joplin and Garcia died. Hank Williams died on the move, on tour, somewhere between Tennessee and West Virginia, his final day a mystery and a country song in and of itself. Johnny Cash had an epiphany while trying to kill himself in a cave. Ray Charles went to rehab. Jeff Tweedy, too. And now Johnny B?

"And on the eve of your first tour, a few weeks before your record drops," Colonel Randy says. "But luckily," he nods to Ricky's dad, "we have a backup plan."

Everything stops: the crying, the chatter, the whispers.

"Sandy is now part of DaWestSidaz," he says, beckoning her forward. "Welcome to the band," he says. She shakes his hand. She looks at me and smiles.

What Would Jimi Hendrix Do?

Rehearsals go poorly. We all miss Johnny B, and Sandy has trouble learning the steps. She's shorter than Johnny, and the choreographers keep making adjustments, conferring in the corners with red faces and dark looks in their eyes. Plus, me and DeJuan are so distracted that we can barely lip sync, miss all our marks, and keep bumping into each other.

Jasper stands near the back of the room, doing lines off the back row of seats and shaking his head at every mishap, giggling like a crazy man.

We take a break so the choreographers can talk to the Axe Body Spray and Sierra Mist people, tour sponsors, to see if there's any way to postpone opening night. We drink bottled water and stand around, wondering what will happen to Johnny B, what kind of contract our parents signed when they filled out the original application. This is where they're supposed to see the big payoff, and nobody wants to let anybody down. Even here, in the bubble of the academy, we know that the stock market has crashed, times are bad.

Ricky plays his role: "Come on, gang! Adversity is just opportunity spelled different! The harder the challenge, the greater the glory!"

Sandy walks up to my left. Beads of sweat are forming on her face like they were drawn there by CGI wizards.

Her eyes are brown with flecks of green, her face the warm caramel of Springsteen's famous Fender guitar. "Hey," she whispers. "What's the deal with this jackass?"

Jimi Hendrix did his greatest work with two guys who would go on to make no significant music for the rest of their lives. He blew through an entire career in ten years—from sideman to Little Richard and King Curtis to phenom to underground legend to superstar to dead legend. The problem with being a true rock historian is that it gives you, as they say in Spinal Tap, too much fucking perspective. This could be our only chance. I could be Andrew Ridgely to Ricky's George Michael, a Pip to his Gladys Knight, one of those poor motherfuckers who was dancing around behind Shannon Hoon in that Bee Girl video.

"How's your brother?" I ask.

She purses her lips. "Addicted to the Internet?" she says. "Please."

Jasper blows smoke out of his nose, a long plume that extends fifteen feet into the air, hangs, rearranges itself into a Fender Stratocaster.

"What are you looking at?" Sandy says.

I almost tell her, then I regain my sanity and shake my head. "Addicted to the Internet," I say. Jasper holds his fingers up, sticks his tongue through the V, and humps the air.

"Okay, team!" Ricky says. "Let's really nail it this time!"

Sandy takes my hand, squeezes, and we take our marks.

———

What Would Joe Strummer Do?

We're in my room, listening to *London Calling*. Jasper is doing bong hits and I'm playing Pac Man on my iPhone.

"It just ain't rock and roll, mate," he says. His accent is kind of a cross between Bono and that Geico lizard tonight.

"We're doing what we can, man," I say.

He takes a hit and blows the smoke at me. It's odorless, and just like Jasper himself, might not even exist at all. I consider again that I may be going crazy.

"So what the fuck am I supposed to do?" I say.

"Rock out, mate," he says, in that Keith Richards kind of way that means nothing and everything, like the Dalai Lama dispensing the most profound wisdom in a three-word sentence. Rock out, mate. And it does sound clear. It does sound wise. Of course I should rock out. What would Robert Plant do? He would rock out. He would rock out in such a legendary way that this pit stop, this prefabricated, lip-sync private school would be just a blip on the radar, an amusing anecdote in a *Rolling Stone* feature, like Bon Scott getting kicked out of the Australian military or Mick Jagger dropping out of the London School of Economics.

"I swear, Jasper. Sometimes I think I get a contact high from just being around you," I say.

He snorts and smoke erupts out of his nose and ears, two long chains that dissipate into musical notes. They hang in the air for a second and then they're gone.

"Sometimes I think you're right, mate," he says, and then vanishes into thin air.

A knock on my door. I bolt out of bed, throw on jeans and a T-shirt. I open the door and step back when she walks in.

"Okay," Sandy says. "We have to talk." She puts a hand on my wrist and my heart slams like a Keith Moon solo. I take a seat at the desk, put my iPod on shuffle, and hope the old Van Halen doesn't pop up.

"What's that?" she says. "That's like Beck, but a little more funky."

"Joe Strummer," I say. "The solo stuff, near the end." Strummer is singing about growing old.

"It's nice," she says. "That voice. It's real, you know?"

We listen for a few minutes. I can't believe this is happening. She looks at my bulletin board, the posters along the wall for the Band, the Clash, the Rolling Stones, the Faces. "What's this?" she says, pointing to the two framed songs.

"My mom," I say. "She was a songwriter."

"No shit?"

"Yeah." I'm warming up a little bit. Maybe she would understand. Nobody here understands but Jasper. "She was good, too. Both of those? Sold to Neil Sedaka. I mean, it's not like Springsteen played them or anything, but still…"

She traces the line of the notes up down up down. "That's amazing," she says.

I get a lump in my throat and pinch myself extra hard to stop from crying.

"Anyway," she says. "Way I see it, if DaWestSidaz is gonna work out, and I mean even a little bit, it's gonna be me and you make it happen."

I nod, follow the line of her sweatpants up her calves to where they cling tight against her thighs. She's wearing a tiny shirt with the Academy logo, her belly snare tight and rippled with muscle. She picks a CD out of the stack of DaWestSidaz demos sitting by my stereo.

"This thing?" she says. "Needs some fucking work."

When he was twenty, Joe Strummer left the 101ers, a band he had started with his art-school buddies and which had a local hit with "The Keys to Your Heart." He had seen the Sex Pistols and knew in his gut that punk was next. He wanted to be next. Strummer was a middle-class kid, not the working-class punk so many would assume him to be. One day he was there, the heart and soul of the 101ers, the leader of an underground art rock movement, and the next he was gone, lead singer of the Clash, punk revolutionary tight on Sid Vicious' tail. When he was playing Shea Stadium, I'm willing to bet he never thought about those poor 101ers, crashing in some London squat. He had a hundred thousand people right in front of him waiting for every chord, every yelp, every punk anthem about Sandinistas and white riots and London burning. He never looked back.

"We didn't even write any of those songs," I say. "It's like, I don't know, I guess I knew this coming in, but, it's like we're not even a real band."

She puts a hand on my leg, pulls the moleskin notebook from the back of her sweatpants. "That's what you and me are gonna fix," she says.

———

What Would Marvin Gaye Do?

"What do we have here?" Colonel Randy shouts. He waddles into the studio, jowls flapping and hands waving. Even though it's two in the morning, he is still dressed in his full suit. He rips the guitar out of my hands, grabs the lyric sheet from Sandy. "Unauthorized use of Academy facilities is forbidden by the terms of your contract." His voice is calm, almost amused.

In the back of the room, Jasper makes guns out of his hands, fires at will. "Wanker wanker wanker," he says.

"We're just working on some teamwork," Sandy says. "Some vocal reproduction issues."

"Really?" Randy says. "Where's the rest of the team, then?"

"On their way," Sandy says. She's not scared at all. She's smiling, calm.

"Jaysus," Jasper says.

"Kiddies," the Colonel says, his tone paternal and condescending, "I've been around this block before. You remember what happened when Donnie Wahlberg decided he wanted to write his own songs? When he starting thinking he was an artist and not a performer?"

Of course we remember. This event is covered in fully half of our Academy classes, mostly under the guise of Longevity/Big Picture and Band Decision Making.

"There's nothing wrong with being a *performer*," he says. "That's what we make here. We make performers. Performers make money. You think Timberlake was worried about writing his own songs when he was here?

I've never seen anybody work harder in Dance *or* Charisma classes than that kid."

"We were just…" Sandy starts.

He holds the notebook up like it's a rebel constitution. "I know what you were doing." He reads the lyrics, then folds up the sheet, stuffs it in his breast pocket. "Do us all a favor, kids," he says. "Stick to the script."

When he was thirty-one years old, Marvin Gaye recorded "What's Going On." He had never created anything like it. Neither had anybody else, and Barry Gordy, the president of Motown, refused to release the single, calling it unmarketable. Gaye had been Motown's hitmaker, their Timberlake, Madonna, Beyoncé. But he had also been in a deep depression since the death of his duet partner Tammy Terrell, and he had come to believe that the hits he'd been cranking out for Motown were pap, irrelevant to the social change he saw all around him, to the damage he saw in his brother, home from Vietnam. He followed his head and his heart and he made one of the greatest albums ever recorded.

Security has shown up. Like everything else, they're slick and costumed—four guys with varying highlights, ripped pecs, and Under Armour tank tops with "Security" stenciled across the back.

"A problem here?" says the head guy.

"A misunderstanding," says the Colonel. "Now why don't you escort our students back to their rooms. And kids," he says, "let's make sure this doesn't happen again."

What would Sid Vicious Do?

Despite what most people think, the Sex Pistols weren't a *real* band. By real, I mean what most people think of as real—John Lennon meets Paul McCartney when they're fifteen, Jagger and Richards bonding over Muddy Waters albums on the train. They were an *arranged* band, a Frankenstein thing created and brought to life by Malcolm McLaren. Vicious wasn't even in the original band, wasn't remotely interested in learning how to play an instrument. He was chosen to be Johnny Rotten's buddy, but even more so because he looked right, acted right, had built up a reputation on the punk scene. So what's the difference between the Sex Pistols and DaWestSidaz?

Well, they did play their own instruments. And once they got started, it was pretty clear that they were at least acting of their own accord—it may have been McLaren who put Vicious there, who wound him up and pointed him in a direction, but the rest of it, the "live fast die young and bury me in my boots and motorcycle jacket," was all Vicious himself.

So why am I sitting here in the dressing room, frozen, embarrassed? This is supposed to be the best day of my life—our first concert is sold out, our single is the featured download on MTV.com, the album is popping up the iTunes charts faster than a Tommy Iommi guitar solo. I've been training for this day ever since the gray afternoon when my mother dropped me off at the Academy five years ago. Then, I was a chubby, scared little boy who had never been outside Scranton for longer than two days and studied

Exile like it was the snarling, barrelhouse baby of the Bible and the Koran. Now, sitting here with Ricky, DaJuan, Lionel, and Sandy, all of us being worried over by a small armada of Academy make-up and hair artists, even with Sandy's glorious thigh rubbing up against mine, I feel like nothing's changed at all.

Ricky finishes make-up and does pushups in the corner. DaJuan goes over a few late moves with the choreography people. Lionel is texting somebody, giggling and nodding his head. Sandy's hair takes longer than the rest of us, naturally, and she sits patient and regal, like she's been doing this her whole life, like this is just part of getting out of the house in the morning.

We are outnumbered. There are three hair people, three make-up artists, a make-up assistant, a nail specialist, two wardrobe consultants, three choreographers, two choreographer's assistants, a few people who seem to be assisting the assistants, the Colonel, the MTV people, the people from the movie tie-in they won't even talk to us about yet, the Under Armour people, Frito-Lay people, Sierra Mist people, three people who are rumored to be representing Ryan Seacrest Productions, and all the rest of the roaming iPhoned army that's pacing around near the east side of the dressing room, where we hear cell reception is best. It's something like forty of them to five of us actual WestSidaz. Is this what it was like when the Stones went on Ed Sullivan?

I look over to ask Jasper that exact question but he's limp on the floor, his bandana tied around his arm, needle sticking out. A vomit puddle extends from his mouth, and his legs are twitching. Overdose. Again. He'll come out of it in a few minutes.

"Fabio. Faaabioooo…" Sandy pokes me right on the nose and I jump. She pulls me into a corner, puts a hand on my shoulder. "Are you nervous?" she says.

"It's not that."

"What, then?"

"It's just all this…" I look over at the make-up people, the Frito-Lay people, the Colonel patting the Under Armour guy on the back. "It's not very, you know, rock and roll."

"Are you joking?" she says. "None of this has been rock and roll, not any of it, not from the moment your mother wrote that first check. You're smarter than that." She slows down a little, softens her voice, places both hands on my shoulders. "We're DaWestsidaz and we're keepin' it real…" she sings the first line of the first song on the album. "And besides," she says, "we got our song, right? We show them how we can do, and then things are different from here on out."

When she says it, I almost believe it.

"Now go on over to hair and get your shit together," she says.

What Would Rod Stewart Do?

Everything goes perfectly. We're hitting all our marks. The production is seamless. The crowd, a carefully selected mix of tween and teenage girls of every stripe and color, hasn't stopped screaming since Ricky walked to the lip of the stage and lobbed his T-shirt into the tenth row.

It's exactly what we've been working for every day of these past five years. Ricky commands the crowd. Me and DaJuan and Lionel don't miss a step. Sandy is electric. During the fifteen-second water break between "Text Me Baby" and "Boardwalk Luvin," it hits me: she is our Timberlake, not Ricky. We're all going to be Pips, Animals, Impressions, Wailers, Supremes, Double Trouble, the Revolution, the Funky Bunch.

"Boardwalk Luvin'" is Sandy's feature song. It's a slow burner, plenty of space for her to melisma up and down the scale. She hits every note, even picks up a bouquet that's been thrown at Ricky and hands out flowers one by one to the Special Olympics kids who are lined up in the first row of stage right. She walks slowly back toward the stage, gives me the sign, turns and shouts "Stop!" It takes the sound guys a fraction of a second to cut the backing vocals and the instrumental tracks, and then everything is quiet. If she wasn't such a pro, if this was anybody but her, this would look like what it is: a glitch, a deviation, a very public breach of contract. But because it's Sandy, because she has it, has been born with it, the whole thing seems like part of the show, as scripted as the dance steps and faux dramas we've already playacted through the first six songs.

She stands at the stage lip, breathing heavy, looking like she's just fended off a pack of dragons. She tosses her hair and the crowd goes crazy. The sound is shrill and urgent and solid, like the air has been replaced by a wall of shrieks and whistles and sobs.

"We got a special surprise for you tonight, people," she says. "A brand-new WestSidaz tune from the songwriting team of Fab and Sandy." She pulls me by the wrist and the wall of screams gets even louder. It's like being underwater in an ocean of noise. It's the greatest sound I've ever heard.

Somehow, I have a guitar in my hand. Sandy is counting down. I hear the Colonel shouting directions offstage. I look over. He is sawing his finger across his throat. The look in his eye is pure hatred. Next to him, Jasper pogos like he's in the front row of the Ramones at CBGB. The lights dim and Sandy leans over, whispers "sing" in my ear, and kisses me on the cheek.

"Ain't no hour don't go by," I sing. My voice is creaky and thin without the backing tracks. "I don't think about you." The lights come back up. Somebody somewhere—maybe the Under Armour guy for all I know—has made a decision to give us enough rope. Sandy pats her tambourine and I play my chords and sing and that ocean of screams is gone and in their wake it's like negative sound, amplified quiet.

By the third verse I know that it's a terrible song and I am no singer. By the fourth, I can see people trickling down the aisles, mothers shepherding their daughters, groups of tween girls in threes and fours. Maybe this has been happening all night long. Maybe not.

There was a period of time when Rod Stewart was the lead singer for the baddest rock band in the entire world. He was twenty-five and fronting the Faces, the one group in the history of rock that could be called a legitimate blood brother to the Rolling Stones. They played a gutbucket blend of blues and rock—fast and relentless and wonderfully sloppy. They were decades ahead of their time and Rod Stewart was at the microphone.

I remember what Jasper said: "Rock out, man." I bring my vocals up a notch and I'm almost shouting, pushing my voice out to that back row, a Springsteenian rock-and-roll preacher here to heal the sick and the musically malnourished.

Sandy puts a hand on my shoulder, raises an eyebrow.

Rod Stewart could have taken the Faces anywhere. They could have been the Animals. They could have been the Clash. They could be the Rolling Stones right now. Instead, Rod Stewart became Rod Stewart. He made one classic rock album and then set about destroying his legacy with disco and sappy ballads.

Sandy whispers and all I can feel is her breath in my ear, her hand on my back.

Rod Stewart has been linked to a series of models and actresses. Britt Eklund, Kelly Emberg, Rachel Hunter. Rod Stewart has mansions the way I have hooded sweatshirts. When Rod Stewart dies, his songs will sing out from every radio in the world.

I stop playing the guitar, cut my vocal right in the middle of the last verse. I estimate I've been playing for about a minute. Sandy is waiting.

"Just playin', y'all!" I shout, and the roar returns. "Let me bring out the rest! Of! Da! Westsidaz!" Ricky, DaJuan, and Lionel come running out. Lionel gives me a look but Ricky is all business. I hand over the microphone and he struts to the lip of the stage. Sandy is on her spot. Dajuan and Lionel are beaming.

I was terrible. The song was awful. All I can feel is a whooshing, everything coming out of me until I'm empty inside. But I'm on my mark. Ricky counts down and I'm doing my steps. I'm singing, lip syncing. I'm throwing Sandy and she is landing. I'm a musical personality entertainer. The crowd is going crazy. I look backstage, where Jasper was pogoing only a few minutes ago. He's gone.

SO FUCKING METAL

THE BUS IS TWENTY minutes late, so Dad runs over to the UniMart for more cigarettes and Uncle Rash limps over to the liquor store. "Stay here," Dad says. "Don't let that fucking bus go any-fucking-where." I turn up the volume in my headphones, watch people straggle into the Goodwill or the Chinese takeout. They stare but I don't mind. People stare. It's a thing they do when you look like me in a place like this.

I've only been metal for about a year, but already my hair is longer than Dad's or even Rash's, longer and more metal than the kids who stand out on the corners smoking before school, more metal even than the guy in Pyl-Dryvyrz, which is pretty much the only metal band worth seeing around here. Or at least that's what Dad says. Uncle Rash says no metal in Central Pennsylvania is worth the drive, but he could be talking about his four DUIs more than he's talking about metal.

One thing I've learned living with Dad and Rash in this past year: a lot of times Uncle Rash seems like he's talking about metal but he's really talking about Uncle Rash.

Three jocks get out of a brand-new Prius and head for the takeout. "Nice tits," says the main one, a kid named

Andy who plays basketball or football or something with lots of homoerotic collisions.

"Fuck off," I say. It's true, though, that I have nice tits. Confirmed by no less an authority than Uncle Rash himself. That was the last time I saw him and Dad in a real fight.

"Freak," Andy Football says.

"Normal," I say back at him. Another thing I learned from Uncle Rash: almost any word sounds derogatory if you say it in the right way.

I light a cigarette, blow the smoke at their backs, and turn up the Black Sabbath in my ears. Rash is hobbling back from the state store, sipping from a plastic bag shaped like a bottle of wine, a few more bags slung across his back. He's whistling and doing the thing where he looks up at the sky and he's walking fast for a guy with a prosthetic leg and he's veering straight across the parking lot, not looking where he's going at all, and cars are stopping, drivers making hand gestures but nobody honking or even saying anything because Rash is overweight with a plastic leg and a scar across his forehead and long greasy salt-and-pepper hair, but he's so totally metal that everybody just knows not to fuck with a guy who looks like that.

"So. Fucking. Metal," I say under my breath, on the exhale so the words come out in a plume of smoke. It's so much better being metal than what I was before, better to scare people away than follow them around begging for scraps. Better to wish for nothing than hope for some kind of bullshit Harry Potter invisible door that's going to open up and make everything awesome all of a sudden, make you popular and normal, make your mother stay on her meds, dress her age, come home for dinner and leave after breakfast and go to sleep in between.

Rash is magic in his own way, so metal that normal people really are like Muggles, boring and straight and scared shitless while he walks straight through intersections drinking wine from a bag on his way to the Ronnie James Dio Memorial Concert in New York City.

"The fuck you starin' at?" he says.

I roll my eyes like I'm sick of him.

He offers me the wine bag and I shake my head. "Your old man won't be back for a few minutes," he says. "Long bus ride, CB."

This is solid logic, but I roll my eyes again and groan and skulk off to look in the windows of the Goodwill. The jocks come back out and I sidle over toward Rash. They get interested in the storefront of the Laundromat, stay real quiet, work their way back to the Prius.

"Fucking normal," I say.

"Fucking normal!" Rash shouts. Then he barks a little bit, scuttles toward them, and they're piling into the car, moving as fast as that hybrid will take them.

"Fuck was that about?" Rash says.

"Just some assholes. From school."

"When you gonna get out of that scene, man?"

"I'm sixteen," I say.

Rash rubs his beard like he's contemplating, fact checking. "I suppose," he says.

Dad shows up with a bag full of cigarettes and barbeque chips. "Bus here yet?" he says.

127

Rash stares at the empty parking lot. Dad stares at me.

"No," I say.

"We missed it?" He's starting to lose it already and I rub his back, give him the sign that he needs to dial it back a notch. I wonder how much he's had to drink, if he did anything else.

"It's not here yet," I say. He plops on the ground, his legs askew, and lowers his head to the pavement. Packs of Marlboro Reds and Herr's chips scatter on the sidewalk. He lowers his head to the ground—bump, bump, bump—steady and hard enough that when Rash finally yanks him up by the hair, there's a crosshatch skid mark on his forehead, red and angry and vaguely sinister in the most metal possible way.

"We're fine for the concert," I say. "Long as the bus gets here before, like, two. That's a half hour away."

Rash makes a noise like a groan and a growl all at once. A thing he does. Dad rubs his forehead and lights a cigarette, takes a pull from Rash's wine. We all stare at the empty parking lot, the places where we think the bus might arrive. People come in and out of the supermarket and I wonder what Mom's doing now, if it's something normal, something like normal people do, if she was really able to get it together on her own and maybe she'll send for me soon or that was just bullshit like everything else.

"You remember that time he brought that whole girls' soccer team back to the hotel?" Rash says.

"Holy shit," Dad says. "London."

"Manchester," Rash says.

"England anyway," Dad says.

"And everybody got their share, right?" Rash says. He elbows Dad and looks like he wants to share something dirty, but Dad is busy digging around in his cigarette pack. "That's how he was."

"You can say what you want about RJD," Dad says, "but he was a fair man."

I roll my eyes. I've heard a thousand variations on this theme since the news broke that Ronnie James Dio had stomach cancer. The death announcement three days ago just made the contractions come faster. In the past two days, I swear I've heard more anecdotes, have—no shit—more straight-up information about Ronnie James Dio, former lead singer for Rainbow, Black Sabbath, and the cleverly named Dio, than I do about the current location and condition of my own mother.

"Clarabelle," Rash says, "not many people know this, but Ronnie James Dio had perfect pitch."

"Jesus Christ, can you call me by my fucking name?" I say.

"Could hear a song and then play it on the piano, like, right away," Dad says.

Ronnie James Dio is dead. My mother could be anywhere. She could be dating a rock star, could be a legal secretary again. She could be working as an escort, or, if things are really bad, turning tricks. She could be just as dead as Ronnie James Dio. I wonder if we'd even find out. I wonder who would tell us.

"He ain't shittin' you, CB," Rash says. "The guy would make you cry, some of the stuff he'd play at a sound check or whatever, sitting around the bus, in the hotel. Was a talented guy." He cuts himself off quick, makes the groan/ growl sound again.

The bus pulls up in a rush of exhaust and we settle into three seats. We take up a full row each, because we know nobody will sit with us, metal as we are. The driver looks like he wants to say something about Rash's wine bags and Dad's lit cigarette, but he thinks the better of it, and we pull out.

Dad and Rash both drink enough that they fall asleep and I watch the Pennsylvania mountains roll by, one after another after another until eventually I start to think that we're not fucking up the planet as much as they say, can't be, if this many trees are all doing just fine right here on the way to New York City. We stop in Hazleton and then Scranton and pick up more people loitering purposefully outside Chinese restaurants until the bus is completely full. The lady behind us is normal and Asian and probably not going to the Ronnie James Dio Memorial and I hope I packed enough make-up on that she can't tell I'm half Chinese. A half hour outside Scranton, she finally taps me on the shoulder. "They okay?" she asks. Her eyes scan Dad and Rash, passed out and snoring. She's got that funny Pennsylvania accent—half Southern, half Amish.

"Yep," I say, and turn up my headphones.

"I'm Grace," she says.

I nod, then notice her expectant face and realize I'm supposed to do something here. "Oh," I say. "Sorry. Clarabelle."

"Such a lovely name," she says. Then she points at my piercings. "Why would a lovely young lady like yourself put these things in your face?" She's about forty, with kind eyes and nice clothes. She could be my mother, if my mother stayed on her meds and got a makeover and got her shit together once and for all.

"Fuck you, you chink-ass bitch," I say. My throat clamps up and I feel like I'm going to cry all of a sudden, but she turns around and huffs, opens up her book and shakes her head. I feel bad, guilty, but good, too. Metal.

New York is crazy. Ridiculous. I've never seen traffic like this, people walking everywhere in giant moving packs. All of them seem to understand the traffic directions even though I can't see anything that tells them when to walk and when to stop and where to go. I realize again that I haven't been out of Altoona since I moved back in with Dad and Rash. I look at the sidewalks, the streets, cars and taxis and trucks too big to be maneuvering through all of it. People of all colors, sizes, everything. By the time we're in Chinatown the crowds have changed to mostly Asian and even though I don't want to give a shit, know it's non-metal as fuck to give any kind of shit, I can't help staring, can't help thinking that any one of these middle-aged Chinese ladies could be my mother.

Dad and Rash are awake, finally, grumbling and telling each other stories they already know. I hear variations on Ronnie and James and Dio and RJD and Holy Diver and all kinds of towns in England that I picture, all of them, as that place where Bridget Jones lived, with the narrow homey houses and the rain and the handsome men fighting outside in the street and the group of colorfully eclectic friends who loved her just as she was. I try to put that image out of my mind—really, really not metal—but when they start talking about the tour, it's all I have. The other people on the bus stare and then look away fast, which is a thing people do, and I wonder if that will happen here in New York City, too, and I think it probably won't. For the first time since Dad came into my room with his shirt off, smelling like pot and whiskey and cheeseburger Hot Pockets, crying and insisting I come outside with him and Rash to say goodbye to Ronnie James in the right way, which involved Jim Beam and fireworks and a reading from the liner notes of *Mob Rules*, I get a little excited about where we're going, what it's going to be like to be in a place where everybody is metal, where I'm normal and Dad isn't so edgy and scared of everything and Rash is probably some kind of fucking *Lord of the Rings* sorcerer king.

The bus stops and people gather their things. Dad and Rash both have unlit cigarettes in their mouths so I put one in, too, then I take it out, tuck it behind my ear. Then we're out in the street and the bus is pulling away and the rest of the passengers evaporate into the crowd faster than I ever thought possible and the three of us are just standing there, smoking and looking up at the skyscrapers, looking at the crazy storefronts that have every single kind of meat you could possibly eat, every kind of noodle, every kind of thing I don't even know what it is, sitting right there for you to try if you wanted.

"Well?" Dad says.

I know he means are we okay for time, so I nod, quickly, before he can lose it. I don't know if we'd even be able to pull him to his feet or if he'd just sit there beating his head against the concrete while a million normal people hurried past.

"Let's giddy-up," Rash says, and he starts down the sidewalk. Dad hurries after him and I take one more look around before I step off, feeling like I'm dropping over the side of something I can't even see the bottom of.

At the very first intersection, Rash does his looking-at-the-sky thing and almost gets run over by an old lady in a jeep. He barks and she does it right back at him, then yells "asshole!" Rash stumbles backward and stares at the yellow blur of her vehicle receding in the distance. He trips, falls on his ass, and stays there for a few seconds. Nobody notices at all. The crowd just expands and then falls back together, like a river's current moving over some rapids. Rash sits on his knees and rubs his eyes, shakes his head like he's trying to wake up.

"Not very metal," I say under my breath.

At the hotel, I change into my dress while Dad and Rash suck beers, blow smoke out the window.

"That's appropriate," Dad says. His eyes are watery and red. He looks away and I wonder if he's thinking about Mom or about Ronnie James Dio or if he's so stuck there in his head that he doesn't really think about anything anymore.

Rash nods and looks at my tits and then looks away before Dad notices. "Ronnie James would approve," Rash says. I can't get over the feeling that he's talking about my tits and not my dress.

"Today is a sacred day," Dad says, and hands me a beer.

"Okay," I say. I take the beer and gulp down half of it.

We see more metalheads as soon as we're a few blocks from the memorial. Old metalheads, young metalheads, black, white, Asian. There are a lot of women who look like they're trying to recreate the Whitesnake videos, the one with the red-haired chick crawling around on the hood of the muscle car. A lot more who look like a mummified version of the girl in the video, meth skinny, with fake tits and a Rite-Aid rub-on tan.

Dad and Rash share elaborate handshakes with some of the older guys, nod, grimace with understanding. The crowd is getting tighter and I feel the occasional hand on my ass, the brush over my cleavage. I hold my backpack tight. I've heard there are pickpockets in New York City. I've heard there's everything.

The memorial concert is being held in some park that I only know is not Central Park. We bull our way through the crowds, onto the grass, and stand in a spot near some trees, where normal people have set up blankets and picnic baskets. Normal metalheads, that is, because everybody is in gear—black, denim, Metallica and Slayer and Black Sabbath, Celtic Frost, Manowar, and everything in between. Dad finds a guy in a Holy Diver T-shirt and pulls him tight into a hug.

The guy is young, twenty maybe, kind of cute in a Russian bouncer kind of way, and he nods and then moves along. He looks back at me and smiles, motions to the left. Dad leans against a tree and sighs. He's had a lot to drink and I don't know what him and Rash were doing in the bathroom for a half hour before we left. Rash holds his arms out to the sky, wiggles his fingers. He nods his head like he's just punched in for the day and shotguns a beer. In the distance, we can hear David Coverdale singing about Sliding It In. This is not my kind of metal.

The Russian bouncer guy loiters over by the trashcans, nodding absently and pounding a fist into his palm. Very metal.

"Hey," I say.

"That your old man?" he says.

"Yeah," I say. "My dad, I mean. That's my dad."

"That guy is pretty fucking metal," he says. "He scares me a little bit, you know?"

"He does that," I say.

"Totally rad," he says, soft, like he's talking to himself. "That thing on his forehead. Is that like a Charles Manson thing?"

"No," I say. "He just...he got upset."

He nods like he understands. "Rad," he says.

We stand there for a few minutes, watching the crowd stream in, listening to the concert in the distance.

"I've never been to New York before," he says. "It's fucking awesome, isn't it?"

"Me neither," I say. "I'm CB."

"Duke," he says.

We listen to David Coverdale, look out toward the stage, a tiny thing far away, a slim shorehead just barely visible from this far back in our metalhead ocean.

"This guy," Duke says, leaning over close so I can smell beer and cigarettes and body spray, "is a fucking wanker."

"Wanker," I say. I've been wanting to incorporate words like this into my vocabulary, some kind of secret put-down language, esoteric and cutting and imported from farther away than Philadelphia or even New York. But who would I use it with? Dad and Rash don't even understand Monty Python references, can't talk anything metal that came out after the year I was born.

I follow Duke's eyes to the area behind us, where Dad and Uncle Rash have set up shop. An old metal chick with skintight acid-wash jeans and hair the color of candy corn is leaning up against Rash. His hand is on her ass and his other hand is pouring a bottle of Southern Comfort down her throat.

"And that would be Mom," says Duke.

"Right," I say.

"Let's get the fuck out of here," he says.

Duke's definition of the fuck out of here is closer to the stage. I follow him through the crowd, pushing, tapping, leaning, and scrunching until we're about fifty feet away. This close to the main attraction, there's no talking, no flirting, no tell me about yourself, no making cutting and incisive statements that nobody in Altoona would ever understand—it's just noise. Plain, simple, basic noise. Noise like I've never heard before in my entire life. It's guitars and drums and the bass thumping somehow in my gut, somehow in my heart. It's David Coverdale wailing about midnight and dragons.

People are sitting, standing, dancing, praying. People hug. People mosh. The sun is setting and the entire place is receding into black and white and soft no edges, like I imagine things look in those England memories that Dad and Rash have been whispering over for the past week.

They finish up a song and Coverdale says some bullshit and I'm just about to make a comment about his fakey English accent when the keyboard player starts in with a riff that even I recognize immediately and the entire place goes bonkers. "Rainbow in the dark!" Duke screams. The guy next to us yells "Like a rainbow!" Everybody is on their feet, fists pumping. The guys on our right—a group of forty-year-old metalheads with short hair but badass neck tattoos and gear you can't fake—have their eyes closed, heads nodding along to the keyboards and the drums and the first verse: "When there's lightning! You know it always brings me down!"

Everybody is standing, pumping fists, singing along. The music is so loud it's a physical entity and I can't feel where it leaves off and I start and Duke is singing next to me and I realize that this is it, that I'm through the invisible door and I'm not with the Muggles anymore, don't have to worry about algebra and homework and where I'm going to sit in the cafeteria and whether I'm ever going to see my mother again and all the other stupid day-to-day bullshit that was making me sad and pissed off and more like Dad every single day. I am metal. We are metal.

Duke spins me toward him, leans in, and the next thing I know his tongue is in my mouth. It's rough and thick and tastes like tobacco but it's also nice and I'm kissing him back and we're rubbing each other everywhere, like fake lovers in some kind of sketch comedy show. I can barely hear Coverdale anymore, the audience screaming "Like a rainbow in the dark!" and "When there's lightning!"

I realize this is the first time I've touched somebody since I hugged Mom goodbye at the bus station in Philadelphia. It feels nice. I am trying not to give in to this teenage girl *Twilight* bullshit but I'm melting into him, letting myself go, feeling the music and the *thump thump thump* and Duke pushed up against me all over. Wanker, I think.

Duke takes my head and pushes it down to where his boner is pushing out of his camouflage shorts. When did that happen? The crowd is singing "Like a rainbow" and I'm feeling the grass on my knees, Duke's hand in my hair, and then I think, What? I get a look at his penis—red and insistent, like a pimple that needs to be squeezed. I stand up. I'm still a little woozy and floaty and it takes me a few seconds to get my shit together. When things get less fuzzy he looks younger, fatter. I'm pretty sure his shirt is from Hot Topic, and what I thought were Doc Martens are actually Sketchers.

"What the fuck?" he says.

I push him, hard, in the chest. He stumbles back and falls over a cooler. I turn and walk, push my way through the crowd. Through the old metalheads who are sitting or leaning or lying on the ground, the young ones who are chasing kids or making out, the people who are crying and hugging and singing still, even though the song is over and the band has stopped and there's a ringing in my ears like I'm inside a bell and I'm still pushing and moving until I feel a hand grab me around the waist and I'm looking into Rash's wasted face, kind and angry and so fucking metal that I just start crying and sit down wherever we are, right onto somebody else's blanket, in somebody else's drink, and my ass is covered in Miller Lite or lemonade or something.

I wipe at it, all of a sudden worried about my dress, about what I look like, who might have seen me there, on my knees, fifty feet from the Ronnie James Dio Memorial Concert.

"What the fuck, CB?" Rash says.

Then there's another set of feet near me, black Sketchers pacing in place. I look up and see Duke, looking soft and not very metal at all. His eyes are red and he looks even younger than before, like a kid, like me.

He sits down and puts a hand on my shoulder. "I'm fucking sorry," he whispers. I'm not sure whether he means sorry because of what he did, or sorry because Uncle Rash is standing there looking metal as fuck and almost as confused as Dad. "I don't know what..." he starts, then he swallows, slams a fist into the side of his head, hard, so even over the music we hear the *thunk*, like a bat into fruit. "I fuck everything up," he says.

"Let's all fucking calm down here," says Rash. "Let's think about where the fuck we are."

I flash on my mother. "I am like lost person," she said that day at the bus station. She handed me a soft pretzel and the ticket. "I am try so strong for you."

Her fucking English. We stood there in the bus station looking like two hookers waiting for a john, two mail-order brides waiting for a husband. The bus came and I got on it. And now here I am again, dressed up like somebody else, like everybody else with my ass-kicker boots and my fuck-me dress. All these men standing around waiting for me to do something. Rash makes his growl sound and Duke punches himself in the head again, but I watch his eyes watching a group of twenty-something chicks a few rows in front of us. Dad just sits there, his eyes red and unfocused. The bruise on his forehead is turning purple and it looks like a horn is trying to sprout.

The sun is down now and it's starting to get dark. I look out past the trees and toward the buildings, impossibly high, stretching up and up until you can't see anything but concrete and lights. I don't know how you get out of this city, how you could if you wanted to, how I'll ever get back to Altoona and high school and yelling "normal!" at jocks and not giving a shit what anybody thinks because I'm metal. Everywhere I look is metal, everybody is flying some kind of flag that's been flown for as long as I've been alive. Everywhere there are girls in dresses like mine, hair like mine, old girls and young girls and baby girls toddling around in Slayer onesies who will be teasing their hair up and banging their heads and shouting at the jocks and rolling their eyes and getting down on their knees before any of us know what happened.

Dad is staring at the ground, waiting for somebody, me or Rash or Ronnie James Dio himself, to tell him where to go, what time it is, how to find the bus or the hotel or the tour van, when to load in and when to load out, where to sign on my report card, on the social security check, on the divorce papers.

I look at the crowd. Black. Leather. Hairspray and tattoos. I walk toward the back of the park, the exits, pushing my way through the crowd with elbows and knees and my steel-toed boots. I need to get to a different place. I step on picnic blankets and trays of food and hands and feet. I don't worry about who is ahead of me or who is following or why. For once, I don't worry about anything.

INTERLUDE:
RANDOM HOLIDAY SINGLE

BEHIND THE MUSIC: A CHRISTMAS WISH

ALL I WANT FOR CHRISTMAS is to be left alone. A little downtime. No fans, no press, no lawyers or sponsors or paparazzi lurking in the hedges. No Holiday Specials or Super Bowl shows or benefit concerts. Just some time to regroup, maybe start writing songs again, get away from all this superstar bullshit and back to what got me here in the first place: the music.

All I want for Christmas is to be accepted as a solo artist. The band was great. I loved the band. I put my life into that band. Hell, just between you and me there are a lot of people who would tell you I *was* the band.

All I want for Christmas is for the label to get behind my album. You'd think I was a brand-new commodity, the third runner-up on *American Idol* or something, the way they're treating me. I've been around. I know what it means to get behind the album and I know this isn't it.

All I want for Christmas is for the band to get through this rough patch, for Luke to deal with the kid thing and James to come out of his money funk and Robertson to get out of rehab and still be able to play the goddamn bass. All I really want is to get back out on tour, on the road, where we're comfortable.

All I want for Christmas is one more hit. I know the first one was kind of a fluke—we were like the last band to get picked for that soundtrack, and somebody told me that Cameron Crowe actually hated our tune but his daughter made him put it on—but I know we have a second one in us. Don't tell the label I said this but we're not exactly teenagers anymore. We have gray hairs, man. We're old enough to think about our legacy. About security. I mean, how many great songs did Soul Asylum have? Soundgarden? One more and I think we can make it last, is all I'm saying.

All I want for Christmas is to give back to our fans. I want that guy in his car to hear our song and relax a little bit, forget about his shitty job or his bills or whatever, just totally rock out for those three and a half minutes because that's the dude we're writing for, playing for, that's what it's all about, and that's really all I want.

All I want for Christmas is a chance to do a third album. The songs on the first one, we had been playing them for years. Of course they were tight. Of course there wasn't a wasted word, a phrase that didn't ring true. That thing was beta fucking tested in every dive bar and rock club on the East Coast and most of the Midwest. The second one was a mistake. Maybe we got caught up in it all, went back into the studio too early. Hey—it was the first year any of us could write "musician" on our tax returns with a straight face. We wanted to stretch our wings. In hindsight, the dulcimer was not a good fit. And the one with the choir, that was probably a mistake. All I'm saying is, we're writing again and the new songs are good and we deserve a chance to put them down.

All I want for Christmas is a tour. A real tour. With a bus and roadies and somebody from the label who'll hassle us about doing PR and being on time. That's when we'll know we made it. I mean, I know the album isn't exactly doing gangbusters, but they're playing it in the right places. The right kind of people are finding out. I see these kids at the shows and they *know the songs*. We just need a tour, a real one, to get this whole thing started.

All I want for Christmas is one of these labels to come see us one night when we are really *on*. When Robertson isn't too drunk, when Luke and James are so tight you'd swear they're two guys with one head, when my voice is rough but sweet and the crowd just seems to *get it* and we're grooving like one big sweaty funky organism. Just once, the right guy in the audience, that's all I want.

All I want for Christmas is a chance to slip our demo into somebody's hands. The right kind of somebody. And for them to really listen.

All I want for Christmas is to stop playing Grateful Dead and Allman Brothers songs and get to a place where we can play our own stuff, where crowds will actually come to hear *us* play instead of screaming "Bertha" or "Blue Sky" or "Dixie Chicken" all night like I'm some kind of hippie karaoke jukebox.

All I want for Christmas is a gig. A real gig. Maybe in Dirty Nelly's, with the little stage where the private school kids do shots and make out in the corners. Where people dance and sing along and our friends could check us out live and I'm pretty sure at least half the crowd would know "Sugar Magnolia" or "I'm No Angel" or "Up on Cripple Creek."

All I want for Christmas is for Robertson to get the goddamn bass guitar that will let us form a real band. Well, not a real band. But at least let us play in the basement, blow off some steam, knock back a few beers, and see what it might be like to be in a band, even if we just do it a few times and then decide it's stupid.

All I want for Christmas is some guitar lessons. Maybe like a gift certificate to the Guitar Center, or for that hippie guy whose card is always stuck on the bulletin board at the coffee shop. Just to learn some basics, a few chords, maybe get good enough to play a few Dead songs.

All I really want for Christmas is a guitar.

ENCORE:
ESSAYS

HOW TO LISTEN TO YOUR OLD HAIR METAL TAPES

FIRST YOU'LL NEED TO FIND the box. Usually this will be a milk crate, sometimes a packing box, a gym bag or a backpack or a few balled-up plastic supermarket bags. It will be tucked into the farthest corners available—your basement, your parents' basement, a car trunk, a storage space, as far away as you can get from your current life and still call something yours. There's an overly obvious metaphorical thing happening here—literally digging into your past, through layers of stuff you've supposedly left behind, blah blah blah. Don't let that stop you. Remember that none of what you're looking for was particularly subtle in the first place. And if you never wanted to listen to your hair metal tapes again, if you had truly given up on Def Leppard and AC/DC and moved on to U2 or Coleman Hawkins or Radiohead, you would have thrown the box away.

The box will be dusty and will smell kind of like the old porn or *Cosmopolitans* you searched through as a kid, the magazines that had been thrown away or stacked into corners, waiting for recycling day. Those magazines were like maps to faraway places. Their images of grown-up men and women, articles on stereos, automatic transmissions, makeovers, menstruation, and all the things men and women might do to one another in private loomed like tourist attractions in places you would surely never visit.

You remember now that the hair metal tapes were a part of the next phase, and how little you seemed to learn from that map at all.

The tapes will feel funny in your hand. They are smaller than CDs, more insubstantial than the vinyl you've recently started listening to again. The TDKs with their orange lines, the Sonys' rounded corners and thick purple plastic. The writing is in the hand of Justin Kline, the older brother of a friend your age. Justin Kline is now a doctor, a father of four with a big house in Central Pennsylvania, only a few minutes from your childhood home.

As Journey might have said, you have gone your separate ways.

Read the titles: Mötley Crüe, Saxon, Coney Hatch, Poison, Axe, Riot, Helix, Tygers of Pan Tang, AC/DC, Van Halen, Def Leppard.

Think of how long these tapes have been with you. Fifteen, twenty, twenty-five years? Somehow they made it through high school, college, young adulthood, and now…whatever this next phase is called. Adulthood? Settling down? Wonder how you've managed to keep them. Wonder quickly, then put it out of your mind. There are many things you have not kept hold of—bank statements, receipts, jobs, friends, relationships. The fact that you still have the tape with Def Leppard's "On Through the Night" on one side and the first Mötley Crüe on the other but not your tax returns from 2008 or your college roommate's email address is evidence of something you don't want to think too much about.

Look at them first. "MÖTLEY CRÜE," all caps, written neat with a blue ballpoint pen, the letters leaning slightly forward, edging toward the margins. Umlauts, of course, included.

Justin Kline's handwriting reminds you that file sharing, peer-to-peer networks, and viral marketing are not inventions of the Internet age. Wonder how all this music found its way to Justin Kline. You grew up in a rural backwater, a tiny farming town in the middle of Pennsylvania, three hours from Philly, Pittsburgh, Baltimore, and D.C. Mötley Crüe and Def Leppard were one thing. But how did the Tygers of Pan Tang make their way to Justin Kline's teenage bedroom?

And why did they spell their name with a "Y" instead of an "I"—"tyger" instead of "tiger"?

Remind yourself that there was a lot of that in those days, creative spelling for no reason. Def Leppard and Stryper and Mötley Crüe. There were a lot of umlauts, too.

Remember trying to spell your name with umlauts: Däve Höusley.

Don't play the tapes yet. Live with them for a while. Put them in your house. When guests or your wife ask what you're doing with a twenty-five-year-old Kix tape, say you were cleaning out the trunk and couldn't bear to throw it away.

Share a memory: mowing your parents' lawn, listening to the Kix "Cool Kids" tape with Billy Squier's "The Stroke" on the other side, how you accidentally ran over a frog and then threw up, couldn't bring yourself to collect the guts and blood, the skin that used to be frog, and throw them into the cornfield that abutted your parents' land. How your father had to scoop them up with a shovel and toss the bloody mess into the field himself. How he never said a word about it.

Think about but don't say that you almost wish you were that sensitive now, how you did a similar thing with baby rabbits a few years back in your own yard and didn't even think twice about putting them into garbage bags, throwing them into the front yard for the county to take away with the rest of the trash.

Think that you may have been a better person when you were in eighth grade.

Gather up the tapes and wait until your wife is away for the day. Make sure nobody is coming over. Sit down in front of the stereo and then realize you no longer have a tape player. Look in the closet for a Walkman or a boom box. The car. Realize you have no way to play tapes anymore.

Go to Best Buy or Walmart or Target. There is one within a few miles of your house. Look for a tape player. When the clerk asks can I help you, tell him no and then continue searching. Try another store.

Eventually you'll locate a tape player, a Sony Walkman that looks remarkably like the first tape player you ever owned. This one costs eleven dollars and you find it in a chain drug store, between the writable CDs and the web cameras. It is four times larger than your iPod and can hold approximately 5,980 fewer songs.

Listen to some of the better stuff first—the old Van Halen, the first few Def Leppard albums. You remember these to be a slightly higher quality than the rest of the tapes.

Don't be surprised that you still remember all the words to "Unchained" and "Dance the Night Away," to "On Through the Night" and "Saturday Night (High and Dry)." These things are burned into your brain and you could no sooner forget them, replace these misogynistic and meaningless phrases with real information, than you could change your high school transcript.

Wonder why it is that you've been listening to the second Norah Jones for a year now and you couldn't recite a single lyric from that album. It is clean and new and comfortable and feels like Sunday morning in bed with the paper, but you can't for the life of you remember anything other than the cover photo, Norah looking clean and new and ready to crawl under the comforter with the *Sunday Times*.

———

Remember the videos. The hair. Good god, the hair. The hair was measured in feet, teased, pushed, blown, and stacked into impossible angles, all of it held together with a brick-and-mortar of Acua Net and blind cocaine bravado.

Your own haircut is about as old as these tapes, the only noticeable change a light retreat in the hairline. Almost wish you had allowed yourself some experimentation, back when experimentation was feasible. Your current supervisors would not be amused if you showed up on Monday morning shirtless and wearing leather pants, a fluorescent blond perm exploding over your shoulders.

Move on to the AC/DC. Be surprised. The power chords are simple, basic, but they still pack a wallop. And the rhythm. Is it possible AC/DC was a dance band after all? Realize AC/DC has never really gone out of style.

When did you stop listening to AC/DC? Maybe when you started listening to grunge. It all sounded so important—messy and urgent and concerned. Maybe when you started listening to hip-hop, traded AC/DC's crackle for Jay-Z's bump. Maybe when you stopped living with a bunch of guys and moved in with your wife, started going out less, worrying more, planning and saving and working on the weekends.

Listen to "Back in Black," the beginning part that goes *duh, dadada, dadada* and then recedes with that *da da da da da* thing, the bass drum and the cymbals controlled little crash kicking just under the surface, moving the whole thing along like a riptide—*boom, ching, boom-ching...boom, ching, boom-ching.*

How long has it been since you really rocked, since you lost yourself in anything? Allowed your face to contort, your body to flail rhythmically, your hand to fold itself into the sign of the goat?

Boom, ching, boom-ching...boom, ching, boom-ching.

You are rocking. No thoughts about the mortgage or work on Monday or finishing that story. Just the drums and the cymbals and the guitars riding along the edge and that crazy-ass rasp screaming out nonsensical lyrics. It is stupid and basic and aggressive. It feels really, really good.

Listen to the rest of the tapes, the lesser-known bands that have disappeared forever. Notice how not heavy they sound. When you were in high school this was the heaviest music around. When the Northwest basketball team warmed up to Whitesnake's "Slide It In" it was absolutely terrifying. Now "Slide It In" sounds funny, cheesy and amateur, Pauly Shore to Led Zeppelin's Lenny Bruce.

The further you go into the archives, the more it seems like this. Aldo Nova. Coney Hatch and Kix and Helix. Notice how produced everything is, how slick and bubble-gummy—Poison could be the Archies hopped up on meth, the Ratt tape sounds like a duet between Justin Timberlake and Maroon 5.

A lot of this will sound truly awful to your grown-up ears. It is pop. In twenty years, will today's hipsters be sitting around with their White Stripes and Black Keys CDs spread out before them, wondering at how bouncy, how sophomoric and tame this music sounds?

Realize that that's the real point of this exercise. Of course the music is tame and cheesy. It was, after all, called "hair metal." And it will always have that gauze of nostalgia, the soft edge that comes from growing up with something. Desperate as it was to be dangerous and edgy, with its amplifiers turned up to eleven, freakshow mascara and hairspray and pyrotechnics, your old heavy metal tapes are innocent. Stupid and harmless and innocent.

Just like you used to be.

The lyrics are stupid and profane, at best the kind of thing construction workers might shout at women passing by. Correction: the kind of thing construction workers might shout at women in a cable sitcom or a Syfy movie.

At worst, they were mental water damage, leaking into your young brain and rotting everything from the inside.

Listen to some Mötley Crüe:

Live Wire, night prowler
Lay back and take me inside
You need me now, I'll teach you how
Come on let's go all the way
I need a piece of your action.
Ah huh!

And that's one of the more subtle snippets from that particular tape.

Compare this to the latest Iron and Wine album, which has been in heavy rotation on your iPod for the past several months. Most of those lyrics seem to be about death, backyard burials, preparing for the end of our "endless numbered days."

You are not old, but not young anymore either. Old enough to have a will. Old enough that a few good friends, people your age, have gotten badly sick in the past couple of years.

Review the lyrical options: on one hand, stupid and dangerous sex; on the other, picking teeth out of the grass and spreading ashes through the yard.

Maybe Mötley Crüe isn't so stupid after all.

Don't throw them away. Put them back in the box or the bag or the backpack. Breathe in that musty smell. Put the Walkman in the bag with them, and tuck it all away. You are old enough now to understand that innocence doesn't always come back. It may not be lost, but it is certainly hard to find. That it may happen to come with pounding drums, hairspray, and offensive lyrics just makes it all go down a little easier.

And, eventually, everything comes back in style.

SET BREAK AT THE JORMA KAUKONEN SHOW, STATE COLLEGE, PA

THE OLD HIPPIES HAVE prosthetic legs, MOOSE sweatshirts, Kangol hats pulled backward over flowing gray locks. They are not holding up so well or maybe they are, and they limp, walk, crutch, waddle, stride purposefully onto the sidewalk for a break, a smoke, a little fresh air. They suck cigarettes, cigars, a pipe, sneak behind corners and come back smelling like the Summer of Love. They check the voicemail or the babysitter, the email or Twitter or the newspaper headlines. They shake hands, exchange business cards, talk about the weather or the war, the football or the old days or Jorma.

Jorma's looking good, they say.

Jesus but Jorma can still play.

Remember that show in Philly? We had to steal a goddamn car, drive it all the way back. Swear to Christ. You were there, right?

That wasn't me. I don't think that was me.

They laugh and look up at the college, dark above them. Students circle the old hippies and disperse back to their bars and dance clubs and coffee shops and god knows where. The students are black and white, Hispanic and Asian, wearing hoodies and skinny jeans, little dresses and business casual and anything that says Penn State. They are young and the old hippies seem to barely notice them at all.

The old hippies have lived in this valley for a long time, or a short time, or they have driven in from the mountains, from cabins and campsites, mansions and contemporaries and little American homes like the ones Jack Kerouac may have dreamed about when he was bumming along the banks of the Susquehanna not that far from here. It has been a long time since that westward trip, since Kesey's bus or that summer when Thompson slowed his Harley just long enough to see the spot where the tide rolled back. Long enough to develop arthritis, emphysema, to stop drinking, stop smoking, eat healthy, go vegan, grow the retirement fund, get a haircut, grow up. Or long enough to come to grips with the fact that none of those things were going to happen.

They are gone now, some of them, but Jorma is here. Jesus, Jorma is here in the middle of Pennsylvania, has come over the mountains and into the valley to play his songs again, our songs again, but really Jorma plays everybody's songs and that was always the point, right?

Maybe he'll play "I Know You Rider."

Well, maybe. But you never know.

We never did know, did we?

That's what made it so good when it did happen.

The old hippies know that set break is only fifteen minutes, maybe twenty. Inside, wine and beer sales are on again, something they don't do when the Hold Steady plays here, or the Drive-By Truckers, or any of the bands for the younger people, those rainbow students with their cynicism and perfect skin and credit cards.

The old hippies check watches, yawn, do the math on how long the last set is likely to be, the drive home, how many hours before the alarm clock. They finish up a smoke, a coffee, grab another glass of merlot for the second set, chew a Paxil, wait in line for the bathroom again. The lights dim and then come up.

Jorma will be somewhere else tomorrow night. Philly or Pittsburgh, Scranton or Reading or New York City. The old hippies will be at work, at the bar, the gym, the mall, in front of the TV or the computer, the Bible or *Rolling Stone* or the *Economist*, on the way to the grandkids' house, the hospital, on the road to another show in another town. But Jorma is here tonight. They are all here tonight. They are still here.

DIM LIGHTS, THICK SMOKE

KELLY LEE BOHN WAS our name. All of us. Officially, we were born on January 20, 1964. It said so on Kelly's driver's license, which was about three feet high, made of poster board, large enough that when we stood next to it, the resulting Polaroid could be artfully cut, slipped into a wallet, and handed confidently to bartenders throughout Snyder County, Pennsylvania.

The bars were dim and smoky and smelled, unsurprisingly, of piss and alcohol. They were small and rough and old and thrilling, and we felt like, finally, we had an answer to the question: what the hell is there to *do* in this town?

At the Olde Trail Inn, we watched Skynyrd cover bands and grouped into corners while the high school sports heroes of our youth smoked Marlboro Reds and did shots of Jack until they grew drunk enough to go out into the parking lot and fight. At the Selins Hotel Bar we played AC/DC on the jukebox and honed our skills at shuffle bowl. At Bots Café, we watched students from the nearby university and realized that we were "townies," that no matter how we looked or dressed or scored on standardized testing, to these students, a few years older and similar in nearly every way, we would always be townies.

We went off to college and found new dive bars. In these bars we sat and talked about girls and music and school with our classmates from New Canaan, Connecticut, and Richmond, Virginia, from Conshohocken and Long Island and every part of New Jersey.

They had a different relationship with the dive bars, these children of suburbia. Their eyes adjusted slower to the cavern lighting. They asked first for Heineken or Amstel Light and were genuinely surprised when the bartender shook his head and pointed at the taps. They avoided contact with the locals, men in baseball hats bearing the names of tractor companies, dressed in work-worn clothing, trailing cement dust and exhaustion. Of course we recognized these men. We had grown up with their sons, many of whom were in the rapid process, back home, of becoming bar men in their own right.

Meanwhile, our new friends, these kids who were so worldly, who owned *Upstairs at Eric's* or *Birth of the Cool* to our *Destroyer* or *For Those About to Rock*, seemed to barely notice the locals at all. They breezed through the barroom, past the shuffle bowl machine and the jukebox, high-fiving and wearing pants that fit in a way that ours didn't, button-up shirts not made from flannel. We watched and we wondered and we drank and smoked and did shots.

In the back of our minds, we knew that we were different, and the neon of the dive bar revealed it like a black light: our new friends were slumming; we were home.

Near the end of college, we lived at the beach for the summer. Here, we stood on the decks of bay-front bars with the rest of the summer help. We met new friends from farther down the coast, and we learned how to crack crabs, to de-vein shrimp. We learned that it was fun to drink out in the open, by the sea, the sun shining in our bleached hair, turning our pale skin pink and then a rusty, lager-colored orange.

We learned, sooner than we would have thought, to hate Jimmy Buffett. We learned that crowds got to be too much after a while, that there were always going to be groups of people who were better looking, more interesting than us, people who seemed like they were born on these deck bars, who knew what the good kinds of tequila were, whose skin turned brown instead of red.

And so we found the dive bars. Billy's, Rosko's Reef, Pirate's Cove. These places were smelly and dark and immediately familiar. We gossiped about our summer jobs while we watched the bar men grouse into their beers. We realized this was the second time we'd moved, only to find ourselves right back at the dive bar. This said something about us that we'd rather not think about, something backward and clannish and maybe permanent, something that would be as hard to get rid of as bad teeth. So we sat at the bar and nursed our Budweisers and smoked our Marlboro Reds, and we didn't talk about it.

———

After college, we moved to the city in search of employment. We usually did it in that order because the only thing we knew about our impending professional lives was that we couldn't do whatever it was we were going to do in Central Pennsylvania. We found jobs, places to live, new friends who went drinking on Friday afternoons with their ties still on. We went to cigar bars, martini bars, wine bars, Irish pubs, dance clubs, rock clubs, other kinds of clubs that we weren't even hip enough to understand.

In the cities where we worked and the suburbs where we lived, we found the dive bars. Hank Dietle's Cold Beer, a Prohibition-era roadhouse sitting wonderfully, directly across the street from Bloomingdales. Dan's Café, where the bartender answered the request for a jack and coke with a bucket of ice, a half pint of whiskey, a can of off-brand soda, and a glass. Hell—an appropriately named basement two levels below a dance club called Heaven—where punk blasted from the stereo and none of the chairs had four legs and the bartender had things protruding from her lips and nose well before this was remotely fashionable.

Of course, we flirted with other bars, the big billiards pub and the sleek, clubby lounges. But when the evening grew darker, we found ourselves back at the dive bar, punching hair metal into the jukebox in a non-ironic fashion and making fun of one another in the tones of people who feel safe and comfortable.

———

Some of us got married. We went back home, all of us together again, and celebrated. After these weddings, we went, sometimes in our suits and ties, our tuxedoes, back to our dive bars. Things were changing, but at the Selins or Bot's it was as if time had stood still. The same people in the same places. They shook our hands and bought us shots. You still living in the city? they said. We nodded, took a drink, and changed the subject.

The wives were the first to stop liking the dive bars. It's so smoky in there, they said. My hair smells like an ashtray for a week. I have to get my shirts dry-cleaned if I ever want to wear them again. And why go out anyway, when we have all this wine?

We grew quiet when this happened.

It's just really stupid, they said.

Um, we said, feeling like little boys and old men all at once.

Oh, for god's sake, they said. Go. Just go.

The nights out got fewer and further between. There were responsibilities—jobs and kids. Still, there were times when we found ourselves with a critical mass, enough Kelly Lees to fill up some chipped Formica table in some dark, smoky bar in D.C. or Philly or New Orleans. Although there were executives and lawyers and writers and artists among us, we talked about nothing, or nothing more substantial than the stupid things we'd done. As the nights wore on we talked shit to one another in the shorthand that only works for old friends—cutting and friendly and casual, no hard feelings, just passing the time, just doing the thing we do, the thing we've always done.

Every now and then, one of us would come back from the bathroom—from checking on the wife, the kids, or the email—and we'd look around at the nicotine-stained walls, the dirt on the floor, the pitchers of swill and empty shot glasses, and think, what the fuck *are* we doing? Why *can't* we go somewhere nice for a change? What is it that we can't get out of us, this dive bar thing like a birth defect, like malaria or the herpes simplex virus. And we'd look at the gray in our hair, hear the traffic outside, and realize we really couldn't go home again and wouldn't really want to if we could. But it felt good to do it—at least a little bit, for a little while—in any dive bar, in any town, anywhere in the world.

ACKNOWLEDGMENTS

Thanks first to Dan Wickett and Steve Gillis, the two nicest guys in publishing. Dzanc was the place I was hoping for when I wrote most of these stories (over the course of several years), and I couldn't be more happy/surprised/lucky/all of the above to have wound up there, especially after taking the (really) long way around.

Thanks to Guy Intoci for his careful and insightful editing, and to Jeff Gleaves for working to get this book into as many hands as possible.

Thanks to Mike Ingram, who read early and much worse versions of most of these stories, and whose insight and knack for calling me on my bullshit certainly made them better.

Thanks to the editors who initially accepted these stories and essays for publication: Aaron Burch of *Hobart*, Mike Czyzniejewski of *Mid-American Review* (and now of *Moon City Review*), Richard Peabody of *Stress City* and *Gargoyle* (and official patron saint of all things literary in Washington, DC), Scott Garson of *Wigleaf*, Jason Teal and Nathan Floom of *Heavy Feather Review*, Chris Fink of the *Beloit Fiction Journal*, Matt Bell, who used to be from *The Collagist*, and

ACKNOWLEDGMENTS

everybody at *Quarterly West, Columbia, Yankee Pot Roast, Knee-Jerk,* and the *Summerset Review.*

Thanks to the entire *Barrelhouse* crew—Becky Barnard, Dan Brady, Katherine ("Aca") Hill, Joe Killiany, Mike Ingram (again), Courtney Elizabeth Mauk, Tom McAllister, Susan Muaddi-Darraj, Matt Perez, Sarah Strickley, Dave Thomas, and Liz Wyckoff—for making the editorial side of my life so much fun.

Thanks to everybody who is making books and stories and poems and magazines and websites and reading series and conferences and literary thingamagigs and doing it just because you love writing and want to get the writing you love out into the world. I can't possibly name all of you, but you've made our corner of the literary world a smart, weird, vibrant, friendly, fun place to be, and I'm looking forward to seeing you all there soon.

A lot of these stories are about, as one early reader said, "the parent/kid stuff," and I'm lucky to have a wonderful, supportive family. Thanks Ben Housley for being awesome and full of happy and keeping my eyes open. I hope when you get old enough to read these stories, they don't freak you out too much. Thanks to Mom and Dad for being the best role models I could ever have.

Thanks always to my wife Lori Wieder. It's hard to carve out space in a busy life for this ridiculous pursuit, and it would be impossible without a partner who understands and believes in you (even when what you do with that space is write a bunch of stories about hair metal and/or the band KISS). Thanks, Lori—you're the best and I am lucky lucky lucky.